Advance praise for
Like Spilled Water

"Family obligations, personal desires, and secret lives collide in this tense yet graceful novel about a girl seeking the truth behind her brother's unexpected death."

—Amelia Brunskill, author of *The Window*

"*Like Spilled Water* is an immersive, riveting book. Amid secrets surrounding her brother's death and parents mired in despair, Na finds the inner strength to forge her own path as a teen girl in modern-day China. Liu weaves an inspiring story through compelling characters who must defy societal expectations to lead authentic lives."

—Jennifer Moffett, author of *Those Who Prey*

"Full of suspense and honesty, *Like Spilled Water* is an illuminating and heartrending examination of cultural norms, gender roles, and the complexity of family relationships in China today. Jennie Liu has crafted an unforgettable story of about the transformative power of forging one's own path in the face of so many barriers—I promise you'll be thinking about this book long after you've finished."

—Amber Smith, *New York Times* bestselling author of *The Way I Used to Be* and *The Last to Let Go*

LIKE SPILLED WATER

JENNIE LIU

❀ carolrhoda LAB

MINNEAPOLIS

Carolrhoda Lab®
An imprint of Lerner Publishing Group, Inc.
241 First Avenue North
Minneapolis, MN 55401 USA

For reading levels and more information, look up this title at www.lernerbooks.com.

Image credits: Visualspace/Getty Images (main); -Slav-/Getty Images (texture); Cartone Animato/Shutterstock.com (line pattern).

Main body text set in Janson Text LT Std.
Typeface provided by Linotype AG.

Library of Congress Cataloging-in-Publication Data

Names: Liu, Jennie, 1971– author.
Title: Like spilled water / Jennie Liu.
Description: Minneapolis : Carolrhoda Lab, [2020] | Audience: Ages 13–18. | Audience: Grades 10–12. | Summary: "Na has always been in the shadow of her younger brother, Bao-bao, her parents' cherished son. But when Bao-bao dies suddenly, Na realizes how little she knew him. And he wasn't the only one with secrets"— Provided by publisher. Includes facts about education in China.
Identifiers: LCCN 2019034451 (print) | LCCN 2019034452 (ebook) | ISBN 9781541572904 | ISBN 9781541599321 (ebook)
Subjects: CYAC: Death—Fiction. | Secrets—Fiction. | Brothers and sisters—Fiction. | Family life—China—Fiction. | China—Fiction.
Classification: LCC PZ7.1.L5846 Lik 2020 (print) | LCC PZ7.1.L5846 (ebook) | DDC [Fic]—dc23

LC record available at https://lccn.loc.gov/2019034451
LC ebook record available at https://lccn.loc.gov/2019034452

Manufactured in the United States of America
1-46578-47594-4/23/2020

TO MY FAMILY.

1

Having just finished final exams, my seven roommates and I are crowded in the narrow space between the bunks of our dorm room, singing to the blare of K-pop and dancing around the mess of clothes, bags, and books strewn all over the place. We're supposed to be packing up, getting ready to head back to our homes for the summer break, but the glee of being done for the year is bubbling over us, and we can't stop laughing and tossing the hairbrush-microphone back and forth. I almost don't hear my phone ring over the noise. I bark out to Xiaowen to turn down the music as I ransack my bunk, searching for my phone under the pile of clothes.

I answer the call. It's Nainai, my grandma, but I can hardly hear her. I press my free hand over my other ear and move out into the hall, but the connection is bad. The reception can be spotty in the countryside at home, and I can just see her yelling into her old flip phone as if shouting will smooth out the choppy breaks and static.

I think I hear her say, "Your brother died!"

And now it's me who's shouting, "What?! What did you say?"

But the connection is already broken.

I can't believe I heard right. *Bao-bao dead? How can that be?* I punch in Nainai's number three more times, but I can't get her back.

I dial up Mama, but the call goes to her voicemail. Same with Baba. I try texting them. I wait and wait, sitting against the wall in the corridor with my knees drawn up, restlessly unbraiding and rebraiding my hair.

My roommates and the girls all up and down the hall laugh and shriek and sing as they stuff their bags and fill the trash cans. There's no response and I'm left frantically wondering, *Why don't they answer? Why don't they call me? What could have possibly happened?* Bao-bao can't be dead.

Finally, a couple hours later, my phone dings. It's a text from Mama telling me to get on a bus and come to Taiyuan. That's all she says. Nothing else. I consider messaging back, hammering her with questions, but I know she won't answer them, because she's paid no attention to me so far.

My roommates help me cram the rest of my clothes and books into my bags, and I drag them to the Linfen bus station in a foggy state of mind. I text Gilbert, my childhood friend, to tell him I won't be traveling home with him to our village, that I have to go to my parents in the city instead. He messages back to ask what's going on. I only say something's happened to Bao-bao, the same vague information I gave the girls. I can't say he died.

I can't, because I wished for it so many times.

✦ ✦ ✦

My bus leaves in the late afternoon, and an hour later, it's still crawling in a procession of coal trucks that clog the roads. The smell of exhaust and burning coal seeps into the bus. The air is thick, and the spewing smokestacks of the refineries near the highways are barely visible in the yellowy-gray smog. With the traffic around the cities, the stops, and the transfers, it will be at least a six-hour trip to Taiyuan where Mama, Baba and Bao-bao live. Where Bao-bao lived.

Because of the fug of pollution, I can't tell when the sun goes down or when the day turns to dusk, but by the time night falls we've gained speed. We pass several massive, well-lit Sinopec gas stations with their rusty exercise equipment and billboards with gory images of what could happen in a car accident if you don't take care while driving.

People crowd onto the bus at the stations of towns and small cities. At one stop, a pregnant woman waddles down the aisle. I automatically stand to give her my seat. She smiles gratefully, but moves one step past the seat I just vacated and ushers a little girl in pigtails, who was hidden behind her, to sit down. Immediately, I regret giving up my seat to this *little emperor*. But then I see the mother's protruding abdomen bump against the girl's head when the bus lurches on, and I remember that I was once like that little girl—a first child showered with attention, indulged, until I was pushed aside by a second child. My brother. Who is dead.

What could have happened? I wonder and wonder, questions stopping up my muddled feelings of bewilderment, old jealousies, guilt that I'm not sadder. Was he hit by a car in traffic? Has he been sick? What sort of terrible disease could strike so fast?

The last time I spoke with Mama, Bao-bao was due to take the gaokao, the two-day, nine-hour entrance exam for college, which he'd been preparing for since middle school when my parents whisked him away from Willow Tree Village. That was when he went to live with them in Taiyuan, where they paid to send him to a much better middle school than the one in the village, and then to a high school, which always costs, but even more so for someone without a city resident ID. He'd just finished his final year, and when I talked to Mama, she was taking off three days of work from the scrap metal plant to get him ready for the test. She had been stocking him with test pencils and fresh erasers, buying him lucky red clothes, brewing brain-rejuvenating tea, and cooking all kinds of nourishing foods to take to the hotel where they would stay to be closer to the testing site.

When Mama told me all that, I felt a hardening in my chest and an urge to push the end-call button on the phone, though I could never actually hang up on her. That bitterness is still with me when I reflect on how much they've always favored him, how much they gave him, but now I'm hit by the suffering that Mama and Baba must be experiencing.

They spent all those years preparing Bao-bao for the exam, hoping that he would test into a good university, the only way to get past a future of farming or factory work. They made so many sacrifices—the years separated from us, the mind-numbing toil in the bad city air, all the money spent on his school tuition, books, and tutoring. Even though I am oddly lacking in my own sorrow for Bao-bao, I know Mama and Baba must be submerged in grief, and I resist the urge to keep ringing and texting them to pry out what happened.

●●●

The bus pulls into Taiyuan around eleven at night, but the city still seems awake. Taiyuan is only a third-tier city, but the avenues within the metropolitan area are as wide as highways and lined with businesses and industrial parks, dizzyingly bright with lighted signs of every color. I texted my parents the time of my arrival, but they didn't respond. Now, I get off the bus and enter the vast, dimly lit station, unsure if anyone will be here to meet me. As I aimlessly follow the other passengers into the echoing building, I start to worry about how I'll find Mama and Baba's apartment, since I've only been to Taiyuan once before.

"Na! Na!" Mama's throaty voice chokes out my name before I see her. There she is, rushing toward me across the lobby, through the straggly crowd of weary passengers who glance at her as she flies by them. Her smallness surprises me, as it always does. The last time I saw her was five months ago in our village during the Spring Festival. She was lively and full of plans then, helping Nainai scrub the house and make noodles and dumplings for the New Year feast.

Now, she looks thin as a child, her face painfully pinched. Her hair is a black, unruly frizz in the heat. She reaches out to me and clasps my arms, squeezing them, before one hand slides up to stroke my cheek. She smiles at first, painfully, but after a moment her face cracks, and tears are streaming.

"Mama!" My voice breaks. I've never seen her cry, and my stomach flips with anxiety. She stands sobbing, her head bent in her hands. People stare openly at her as they pass by. They know these are not tears of a happy reunion. My ears turn hot at her public display. I am completely helpless.

"Mama, let's go," I say timidly. I hook my arm through hers and pull her along while my heavy bags bump against my back and hip. I don't know which way to go, but I have to do something to get her to stop crying.

Slowly, it works. She sniffs fiercely, as if determined to inhale her misery, and swipes her face. We cross the bus station, our shoes clicking on the tile floor. As soon as we're outside in the shadows and spills of city lights at night, Mama is recovered enough to lead me toward the metro station. Her tears have stopped and she seems intent on hurrying us there.

We have good timing; the train arrives just as we're descending the steps. Once we sink into our seats, Mama looks at me. Fatigue is still written all over her face, as if she hasn't slept in days. "I should have brought you something to eat," she says with an apologetic grimace.

I shake my head. "I ate." The last meal I had was in the midafternoon, fried bread I grabbed on the way to the bus station. My stomach is an empty pit, but I don't want her to worry about me now.

She sighs, and her shoulders slump like wet concrete has been poured over her. Her round pale face, usually so luminous, is pasty gray in the fluorescent light of the subway car. She looks so old, though I know she is only forty-five. I want to ask her about Bao-bao. I want to know, and my tongue itches to ask, but it's not the right time. I'm too afraid she'll start crying again.

"You're here," she says absently, her eyes vacant. She pats my arm with her hand. I can tell she's still struggling to hold herself together.

I nod, and we fall into silence as the train speeds underground. The silence is like an insurmountable space between us, a void. I fret over it, but Mama is lost in her own thoughts. We get off at the next stop and Mama carries one of my bags as we walk to the bus stop. There's more silence between us as we wait for the bus. I try to come up with things to talk about, but everything that pops into my head seems trivial or might upset her.

I'm glad when the bus arrives. As it grinds through the streets, I see that we're heading toward the outer ring of the city. Finally I think to ask, "Where's Baba?"

"At the apartment," Mama answers. "He just couldn't make it to the station. Oh, he's been so . . ." She blinks furiously.

I squeeze her hand as she clamps her lips together and brings her fist up to her mouth, collecting herself again.

"You're a good girl for coming," she says hoarsely. "We need you."

My heart jumps. They need me. She's glad I'm here. I know it is small of me to think this now, and I immediately suppress the feeling.

"I'm just tired to death." She flaps her hand close to her chest as if asking me to excuse her. "I worked until nine, then ran home to check on your ba. He's . . . not doing well. Not been able to work. I've been doing extra shifts to try to make up for him." She leans toward me, nudging my shoulder with hers. "It's good you're here. You have to help take care of your baba."

The words are like a warning signal. The Baba I saw at the Spring Festival was loud and boisterous, goading Bao-bao and me to set off fireworks, tossing back shots of liquor with the friends we visited, eagerly exchanging information about study schedules and rankings with the other parents whose kids were able to go to high school. What does she mean *take care of him*?

Despite my growing unease, I try to keep my voice steady and calm. "Of course. Now that I'm finished for the summer, it's no problem." I've just finished my first year at vocational college in Linfen. It doesn't offer the traditional academic course of study, but I'm lucky to have found it—and lucky that Mama and Baba agreed to let me go and help me with the tuition, which is far cheaper than a regular college or university. Before I had heard about the school, they had wanted me to go straight to work.

Mama's face clouds briefly, but she says, "Yes. You're done for the summer. Did you do well on your exams?" The lights from the streets flash in her eyes and the distracted look creeps back in before she turns away to the window. I imagine Bao-bao and the gaokao have just shot back into her mind, so I just give a noncommittal murmur instead of a real answer.

The bus mounts an overpass in a tangle of interchanges and now we're on the outskirts of the city, where it's not so bright. Blocks of dingy white high-rises loom in rows and rows along both sides of the highway, clearly visible in the darkness. We lurch and stop several times before Mama gestures for us to get off at a massive complex called Glorious Towers.

Lugging my bags, we file past several identical buildings before we enter one through a dirty glass door. I remember the spartan, grubby lobby from when I came last summer to help them move from the small third-floor apartment of another building to the basement floor of this building—one of the sublevel units that were framed in as an afterthought as a way to squeeze more rents from the property. We pass the grid of mailboxes, the elevators, and flyers covering the walls offering services for remodeling, drivers, "massage."

I follow Mama down the stairs. The air changes. It's cooler, but the subterranean atmosphere is stifling. The wan light has a sickly cast in the long, narrow passageway where I see only a single short fluorescent tube tacked to the low ceiling. I remember being taken aback when I first saw the place last year. Mama said they had to economize and move to an even smaller apartment—so they could afford more tutoring and extra English classes on Sunday for Bao-bao. She worried about how the underground conditions might affect him, but she told herself that he would be at school from seven in the morning to nearly eleven each night, so he wouldn't suffer too much from the dank air and cramped space.

The sublevel is damp and smells of cooking odors and stale cigarettes. Through the unfinished drywall and hollow-core doors, I can hear people snoring, music and videos playing as we weave our way through the warren of apartments. The doors are mostly unmarked, and I can't remember which one is theirs, but Mama locates it and lets us in.

She snaps on a lamp clamped to a cart just inside the door. The apartment is as tight as I remember. There is only one bedroom, and the bed in the main room is in disarray and takes up nearly a third of the space. The cart next to the door holds a hot plate, an electric rice pot, and a small fan that whirs quietly and stirs the air in the room. There are plastic baskets of clothes, books, and other miscellaneous items in another corner, a couple of plastic stools. I look for a spot to put my bags.

Mama reaches for them and piles them on top of the other things in the corner.

"Tired to death!" she heaves again. "I should make you something to eat." She points at some packages of instant noodles stacked on the lower shelf of the cart among some kitchenware and other foodstuffs.

My stomach grumbles, but I say, "Don't bother, Mama, just go to sleep."

Her head dips in agreement, or from exhaustion. "You remember where the toilets are?" she mutters.

"Yes. Don't worry about me. You're so tired, you have to sleep."

She digs around for a nightgown and turns around to change. I'm surprised when she climbs into the bed here in the front room and scoots against the wall to make space for me before collapsing into a heap on her side. Since the bedroom door is closed, I suppose she probably doesn't want to disturb Baba. I root in my bag for my pajamas and put them on before shutting off the lamp and climbing into the bed beside Mama. I position myself so we're back to back, not touching.

In all my nineteen years, except for when I was first born and the two weeks at Spring Festival every year, we have never lived together, and it's strange now to be sharing a bed. I feel her flip around behind me, her breath on the back of my neck. She strokes my hair once before her breathing falls into the steady rhythm of sleep. I lie awake for a long time in the dark.

2

There is no window in the apartment, and I don't hear an alarm, but somehow Mama knows when it is time to get up. I come fully awake as she carefully climbs over me, snaps on the lamp, then throws a shirt over it to soften the light. From bed, I watch as she pours water from a plastic jug into a pot on the burner, drops some tea leaves into a big glass jar, and changes her clothes. She does everything nearly soundlessly, moving like a dreamwalker until she's standing over the pot, staring at the water, waiting for it to boil.

"Mama," I say.

She turns to me, startled for a beat, as if she forgot I was there. "You're awake? Go back to sleep. It's too early."

I sit up, hugging my knees over the sheet. "You're going to work?" Because I just arrived, I want her to stay home. But she worked yesterday, so of course, she has to go in today. It makes me wonder how long ago Bao-bao died, given that she's already back to work.

She nods as she pours hot water into her jar and a big thermos. "Here's water for your tea and for Baba when he gets up." She holds the thermos up before setting in on the ground. "But you don't have to get up now. He won't wake up for a while."

She's leaving me to *take care* of him, so I have to ask. "Mama, is he sick?"

She tilts her head back and blinks at the low, close ceiling, a look of utter despondency. "Yes. Very sick. About what happened."

I toss the sheet aside and swing my legs over the edge of the bed. "But what happened? How did . . ."

Mama's face begins to crumble. She covers her mouth with her hand as a cry escapes her. I jump out of the bed and rush over to her, making apologetic murmurs while inwardly cursing myself for bringing up Bao-bao. It's too soon.

Her steaming tea is on the crowded cart. I find a towel to wrap around it and lead her to the side of the bed. We sit and I press the jar into her hands. "Drink this."

Tears drip into the tea as Mama bends her head over it. She looks like she's praying until she takes several noisy sips.

"What about food? What can I make you?" I change the subject, trying to put her distress further behind us, although I'm still impatient to know what happened to Bao-bao.

"There's nothing here except instant noodles. I'll get something on the street." She is slowly pulling herself together into the efficient, in-charge Mama I know. "You should too. Later, you'll have to go get something for you and Baba." She reaches for her purse, pulls out several yuan, and lays them on the cart. "If Baba's having a . . ." she stumbles for a word, "a hard time, go next door and ask Mr. or Mrs. Hu to stay with him. They're trash pickers and usually finish their rounds by seven or eight o'clock in the morning."

She reaches for the jar lid and screws it over the tea. A moment later she's digging a comb out of her bag and running it roughly through her hair as she steps to the door. "Go back to sleep now. You had a long trip."

Sleep is far from my mind. I'm not tired at all, but Mama stands there with her hand on the doorknob until I slip back into bed and pull up the sheet. Her mouth twitches as if she's trying to put on a smile, but the expression is pained.

She opens the door and clicks off the lamp. Her shape is a silhouette in the faint light of the hallway as she hesitates before going through. "And Na . . ."

"Yes?"

"Don't let Baba harm himself."

She leaves before I can ask her what she means.

◆ ◆ ◆

After Mama leaves I lie in the dark with a panic beating inside me. I tune my ears toward Baba's room. The fan is droning softly, but I hear unsettled snoring from the flimsy door between us. Harm himself? Mama said he was sick, but now I register that she meant sick in the head. Sick with heartbreak.

I tell myself that at least he isn't physically ill. To be sick with grief after a death makes sense. What doesn't make sense is how I feel. As his sister I should be a weepy mess like Mama or immobilized with sorrow like Baba, but about Bao-bao's death, I am inconceivably detached. I know that's an awful thing to say, but Bao-bao and I haven't lived together for six years—rarely spoke or saw each other except for the annual holiday. And in truth, I resented him.

We were close once. Bao-bao was born a year after me, since second children were allowed to families in the countryside if the first one was a girl. Baba was still old-fashioned enough to want a boy. He felt that a daughter is *like spilled water*, since traditionally once a girl marries, she becomes part of the husband's family.

Like most children from the countryside, Bao-bao and I were *left-behinds*, raised by grandparents while our parents migrated to work in the city. Nainai raised us, and when we were sad or angry that our parents left us, she scolded and explained that children were expensive and Mama and Baba had to work to support us—two of us no less—when they could've saved their money to build a new white-tiled house instead.

When Mama and Baba came home for the Spring Festival each year, they showered both of us with gifts, sweets, and supplemental workbooks. They gave us long lectures about studying and demanded to see our graded papers. When Mama saw all my perfect marks and noted my class rankings, she gave me extra talks about helping Bao-bao with school, making sure he did his homework and kept up his grades.

I was proud to help. Bao-bao was quite smart and only a little lazy, and he listened to me. Like I said, we were close then. Many of the children in the village were singletons, alone with their aging grandparents, but for us, having a sibling took away the sting that our parents were never with us.

The summer after Bao-bao finished primary school, Mama and Baba came home to the village unexpectedly. We were both surprised. And even more surprised when they took Bao-bao away to live with them and start middle school in the city. I was thirteen and left behind again, suddenly alone with Nainai, wondering why Mama and Baba hadn't taken me. I was the firstborn, the better student. The one who should have gone to school in the city. If I had been a singleton, it would have been me going with them.

Now in Taiyuan, I hear guttural coughing erupt from Baba in the next room. I quickly set down the bowl of instant noodles I've been eating, grab the tea I made earlier, and move to put my ear against the door. The hacking settles for a moment, but when it starts up again, I tap on the door. "Baba?" I whisper, uncertain whether I should check on him or just leave him alone. My sense of time has been distorted by the windowless room, but it must be late morning. I've been up for several hours already, dressed and waiting.

His coughing stops, but I hear heavy, labored breathing. I softly knock again before I push the door open.

The smells of ash, sour alcohol, and an unwashed body hit me. Light from the lamp behind me steals into the room, which is half the size of the front room. My eye falls briefly on the desk, facing the door, littered with beer and liquor bottles along with several overflowing ashtrays.

Baba, in a dirty singlet and underwear, is sprawled on the narrow cot against the wall. His chest rises and falls, and his eyes flutter as if he's halfway between awake and asleep. The skin of his face is gray-tinged in the gloom. I start to step back and leave him, but suddenly his eyes open, and he's looking at me. His expression is dispassionate at first. He could be looking at a store clerk or a bus driver. But slowly his eyes grow round and his mouth falls open. There's joy in his face, and I swell up inside.

He struggles to sit up in bed. His movements are lurching, and he lists to one side. "Bao-bao! My son!"

My heart shrivels, and I freeze. He's confusing me with Bao-bao. When we were younger people always commented that we looked like twins with our heart-shaped faces and widow's peak hairlines. Last time I saw him, thin hair had grown over his lip, and he'd gained weight from Mama's cooking, but in the underlit room with my hair pulled back in a tight braid as it is, I can imagine how I resemble a younger Bao-bao.

I move toward him. "Baba, it's me— "

He doesn't seem to hear me. Fear is shadowing his eyes now. A low, long wail comes out of him and he pushes back against the wall, cowering like a frightened child. I set the tea on the desk, but my movement rattles him.

"You've come back to . . . too much . . . gaokao . . . all the money . . . fail . . . why!" He is yelling, slurring, blubbering. I can't understand him.

"Baba, I'm Na. It's not Bao-bao, it's Na!" I plead with him, but I stay back, my hands wringing together in a helpless fluster, because I don't know what to do. He just moans more loudly and shrinks farther away. He thinks I'm a ghost. Bao-bao's ghost.

I hear a sharp rapping on the front door. Startled, but desperate to escape this moment with Baba, I run to the other room and fling the door open. A woman holding a bottle of clear liquor pushes me aside and heads to Baba's room.

I shut the door to the hallway, but not before I glimpse several neighbors poking their heads out of their apartments.

Afraid that I'll further agitate Baba, I don't follow the woman back into his room. I stay in the front, biting my thumbnail, listening.

"Pah! What are you yelling about?" the woman scolds loudly over Baba's voice. She clicks her tongue in reproach. "You're scaring that girl—your daughter! Drink this. Here, here! Calm yourself now!" I hear Baba cough again, sputtering on the strong liquor. "Yes, drink up. That's your daughter out there! What's this business of shouting like that?"

Baba's moans begin to die down. Soon he is only sniveling, and the old woman's murmurings become more soothing. A few more minutes pass until all is quiet, and the old woman comes out with the empty teacup and the bottle of liquor. I can see it's been drunk down a few centimeters.

"He's asleep again, but he should have something to eat soon. I'll get my husband to come over here so you and I can go to the wet market."

"You're Mrs. Hu?" She's older than Mama, her hair half gray and her middle thick, straining against a flowered shirt and clashing plaid pants.

She nods. "That's me. Listen, I'm going to put this here." She tucks the bottle of liquor amongst my bags in the corner, hidden from view. "You'll have to give him some later, but be stingy with it until your ma gets home."

"Thank you for coming." I release a shaky breath. "I didn't know what to do."

"Aiyo!" She shakes her head dolefully. "What's to be done? It's terrible, just terrible. Put your shoes on while I get my Old Hu."

She's back in a few minutes. Mr. Hu shuffles in behind her with his reading glasses, a thermos of tea, and some newspapers. After he nods to me, he parks himself on a short stool in the front room.

I grab the money Mama left and stuff it into my purse. Mrs. Hu and I thread through the passageway, up the stairs, through the lobby. Despite the smog of the city, the glare of day hits me as we go out. Cars fly by on the overpass and highways. I have to stop and squint as the oppressive darkness of the sublevel leaves me. Mrs. Hu doesn't stop, and I hurry to catch up as she crosses the plaza of Glorious Towers and exits through the gate.

The wet market is packed. I follow Mrs. Hu as she weaves through the crowd, eyeing vegetables of every color, raw fleshy meats, and grains loaded on tables and plastic bins that edge into the wide alley from the tiny stalls and carts. She pauses every now and again to squeeze an eggplant or examine a tuber as she makes her way to her favorite sellers. I hastily select some eggs and greens to cook for Baba. I'm used to cooking for myself because it's cheaper than eating in the dining hall at school, but my mind's not on the shopping.

I've been replaying how Mrs. Hu handled Baba. She came at just the right moment, saving me from . . . I can't imagine. I don't know what I would have done, what Baba would have done. I realize that she must be closer to my parents than anyone else, and that she is the person to ask about what happened to Bao-bao.

She glances into my shopping basket. "Your baba is going to need something more than eggs to soak up all that baijiu. We'll get some pork buns down the street. And you have to help your mama—get something for her dinner. She's probably not taking any better care of herself than your baba is."

A small piece of pork, more vegetables, and a bag of rice go into my basket. I'm waiting for just the right moment to question her. After we pay and move away out of the alley, I get my nerve up. "Mrs. Hu, my baba and mama have been so upset, they haven't told me what happened to my brother. I don't even know when he died."

My chest tightens as I admit this. It's humiliating that my brother is dead and that my own parents don't think enough of me to explain how it happened. I know they're in a dark hole of misery, and it's selfish of me to think like this, but it's not right that no one has told me anything.

Mrs. Hu's eyes shoot to me before she looks away. "Your poor parents! The worst kind of trouble."

"But what happened?"

She shakes her head, and it seems like she's avoiding my gaze. She moves toward the steamed bun vendor on the cross-street from the alley. I wait patiently as she orders six buns for me and two for herself, but I begin to worry that she isn't going to tell me anything.

Only after we get our buns and step away from the bun seller do I try again. My chest is tight with frustration, but I try to keep it out of my voice. "Please tell me, Mrs. Hu. I don't want to make Mama talk about it right now. It just makes her upset." I try to sound calm and practical. "Who else will tell me if not you?"

Mrs. Hu pulls a napkin out of her purse and swipes the sweat from her forehead and neck. It's nearly midday. Heat radiates from the concrete and asphalt of the buildings, sidewalks, and roads.

"Last Friday, around dinnertime," she says, checking the traffic before we cross the street.

I wait for her to continue, but when she doesn't, I place my hand on her arm to stop her from crossing. "Yes?"

She looks at me for a long time as if trying to decide whether to say more. Finally she says, "It's always noisy in the sublevel after everyone gets off work—the TVs, music, everyone coming and going. Old Hu is a little hard of hearing and he had our TV turned way up, but at some point I heard noise from your parents' apartment. It didn't sound like ordinary arguing. I told Old Hu to shut off the TV for a minute, and that's when I heard your baba shouting, then your ma scream." Her eyes dart left and right as if she's hoping to cross the street and get away from my questions.

"Then what?"

The skin on her face is stretched tight. When she finally continues, her voice is toneless. "I went out to the hallway and knocked on your parents' door. I could hear your ba crying, so maybe they didn't hear me right away. Finally your ma opened the door. She could hardly speak. She just moved aside like a ghost. By then the neighbors were trying to crowd in. I pushed them all back and shut the door, then went back to the bedroom."

She closes her eyes and shakes her head, more of a shudder, as if she's trying to erase what she is seeing. I'm afraid she won't say any more, and I open my mouth to prompt her, but before I do she adds, "Your ba was sitting on the bed, sobbing and rocking and cradling your brother like a small child."

My stomach is queasy at the picture, and I feel sick about my need to know. It's like a morbid curiosity, but I'm unwilling to let it drop there. "Was he already—gone?"

She nods curtly.

"But how? How did he die?"

She swallows, but doesn't answer.

"Mrs. Hu, please," I say.

She lets out a long, low breath. "There was a box of rat poison. It was spilled on the floor, and white powder was all around your brother's mouth."

3

My stomach sours as Mrs. Hu and I walk home from the wet market. She told the story so vividly, I could see Baba coming home from work, going into the bedroom, finding Bao-bao lying on the bed with the rat poison next to him. Baba must've cried out, rushed over, shaken him. Mama would've come in and shrieked to see Baba collecting Bao-bao in his arms, while he yelled at her to call an ambulance even though by then they knew he was dead.

But Mrs. Hu said that there was no ambulance. She had sent Mr. Hu for the on-duty police officer they knew from their trash and recycling rounds. The officer called in the coroner. And once it came out that gaokao results had been published that day, and Mrs. Hu told him about Bao-bao's score, his death was easily ruled a suicide.

"A couple of other suicide attempts by students had already made the news in the previous weeks," Mrs. Hu explained. "Like every year around gaokao time."

The gaokao. The all-important National Higher Education Entrance Exam, which every kid who wants a better future has to take. The brutal test Bao-bao spent the past six years—longer than that, really—preparing for. The test I never got to take.

Mrs. Hu tells me that Bao-bao scored 398/750, too low to even test into a second-rate college in a third-tier city. I'm shocked that he did so poorly and I say so to Mrs. Hu, but she only flips up her hands in a *don't know* gesture.

"What about all the cram sessions and extra classes? The Sunday morning practice exams?"

Mrs. Hu sighs. Her shoulders lift and drop.

"I thought Bao-bao was a pretty good student," I say, still stuck on this, but Mrs. Hu's expression is closed off. It's clear that she's done talking. I remember Mama mentioning some older neighbors who were shidu fumu, parents who had lost their only child, and I realize Mrs. Hu must be who she was talking about. I don't ask her anything more about Bao-bao, figuring that her thoughts must be on her own loss. Still, my mind races with questions.

I remember Bao-bao last winter in the village, sitting hunched over his phone with his earbuds on, shutting the family out, while Nainai, Mama, and I bustled around cleaning and cooking. He didn't seem stressed at all. How could he have snapped so drastically from a bad score? To *kill* himself! What sort of impulse was this?

I know a person can take the gaokao over, although it's only given once a year in June—practically a national holiday, the way the roads shut down and construction work pauses around the testing sites and parents keep vigil all day outside school gates. But another year would have given Bao-bao plenty of time to bring up his score. Did he give up hope of ever testing into a good school? Was he so ashamed of crushing the plans of our parents? Did he so dread the thought of working as a laborer?

The truth is, I have no idea what Bao-bao was thinking, or

what he was feeling. After he left me behind in the countryside, I didn't know him at all.

When Bao-bao first left the village for middle school, Mama used to put him on the phone during our weekly calls. At first, we missed each other and he was eager to talk to me, but soon he was prattling about the special foods Mama was cooking for him, the yogurt drinks Baba bought him, the zoo with the two-headed goat, and the underground metro the city was constructing. After a few months, I could hear Mama wheedling him to come talk to me. He would only say, "Hi, Sister" or "How are you, Sister?" when prompted by Mama until eventually she wouldn't even bother to hound him to get on the line.

Instead, she gave excuses. "He's so tired from school. He's studying, I don't want to disturb him." From Mama, I'd hear about the extra classes Bao-bao took on Saturdays, the special gifts bought for his teachers, his new desk, his rankings in every subject, his favorite study snacks.

It stung that Bao-bao was pulling away from me, and of course, I was envious. He was being pampered as much as any singleton. He was headed to an elite college, a promising career. He would take care of Mama and Baba in their old age. It's terrible to admit that I harbored such an awful bitterness toward Bao-bao, but I'm a tiny bit glad now that he didn't care enough about me to have ever known about it.

✦ ✦ ✦

When Mrs. Hu and I get back to the apartment, Baba is in the front room hunched on a stool beside Mr. Hu, nursing a cup of steaming water. His eyes are bleary and he looks hungover.

Mr. Hu is reading the newspaper to him, but when we come in, he stops and folds it up.

"Here they are," Mr. Hu tells Baba as he rises from his stool. "You see, your daughter, like I told you!" Mr. Hu waves me over to stand in front of Baba.

"Baba, I'm here. I've come to help you and Mama." I know by now not to mention Bao-bao.

Baba's head bobs on his neck and he gives me a mournful, grateful look. "Na! Our little Na. Not so little anymore." His eyes try to focus. "You've grown up!"

I wince at the peculiar way he speaks to me, like he hasn't seen me since I was just a small girl. Fearing he's going to become maudlin, I pull out one of the buns. "Eat this, Baba. Mama said I had to make sure you eat something."

As he reaches for it, he nearly topples off his stool. I move to help him right himself and take his cup away. I can smell the alcohol on him. He tears into the bun and starts chewing.

Mrs. Hu says, "Old Hu, let's go home and eat." She turns to Baba. "Now, no more of this yelling today! You know Old Hu and I have to sleep after we eat or we won't be any good at our recycling tonight." She pats me on the shoulder and ticks her head toward my things in the corner to remind me where she hid the baijiu.

When they're gone, I'm nervous being alone with Baba. He blinks sleepily and sways on the stool while he eats. I don't know what to do with myself and I cast my eyes around for something to occupy me. I take the groceries out of the bag and lay them on the cart, trying to be as unobtrusive as I can.

"Baba, I'm going to clean up your room while you eat. Then it'll be ready for you to take a nap."

He agrees by closing his eyes and ducking his head forward.

I slip into the room with an empty bag. The tiny space is still dim and shadowy despite the circle of light the gooseneck lamp throws on the desk. I empty the ashtray first, then begin placing the empty beer and liquor bottles carefully into the bag so they don't clink.

My eyes run over the room as I work. Posters cover the walls: bands I've never heard of, the basketball players Jeremy Lin and Chen Nan. Textbooks and composition books are stacked neatly on one side of the desk and on the floor. There's a pencil holder with the Harvard logo. The pens are lined up neatly on one side and all the pencils in the other half are sharpened to a point. Two plastic baskets of folded clothes sit under the desk with Bao-bao's school uniform folded neatly on top.

So this was Bao-bao's room. When I helped them move into this apartment last year, we put the bigger bed in here. I remember it took up nearly all the space. Now the desk is here alongside Bao-bao's smaller bed, the old hospital cot with the iron frame Baba proudly scavenged years ago. It's clear now that Mama and Baba gave up their room to Bao-bao. My hand tightens around my trash bag. I can easily hear Mama say something like *Bao-bao needs his own place to study with no distractions.*

I'm examining the papers tacked in rows on the bulletin board above the desk when Baba stumbles in to stand beside me. He has lit a cigarette and takes a long pull on it before tapping the ash onto the floor. I try to smile at him.

"Na, I see you're looking at your brother's certificates." A tormented smile pulls at the corners of his mouth. "Look at this one." He jabs a finger at one near the top. "Best composition!" He moves his hand over the four sheets below it. "And here's his report cards for his first four years. All 97 or above! His class rankings were always good then."

He swings around and gestures at me to shut the door. "Behind there! Look at that. That one was for the art competition he won in middle school. You remember how he loved to draw? How good he was at it?" Baba heaves out a breath and his whole body sags. "We thought he should quit the art elective in high school for more study time. He was on the science and engineering track. Did you know that?" His face lights up for a moment, and I nod, pulling my braid around and absently stroking it while he talks. Although my old jealousy is blistering up inside me, my heart also aches for Baba, so proud of Bao-bao, desperately hanging on to his achievements.

"He quit the art, but we let him do the music for a time, because music helps to develop the mathematical part of your brain. He did piano lessons for a few months. We wanted to get one for him, but there was no space in the apartment . . ."

I tilt my head with exaggerated interest while Baba rambles on and on, repeating all the details of Bao-bao's hard work and talents that I've heard so many times before. But as much as I trying to pay attention to Baba's good memories of my brother, my mind wanders to the question, *With all that rigorous study, how did Bao-bao manage to score so poorly on the test?*

4

The next morning, a Saturday, Mama doesn't go to work, but she doesn't sleep in either. I make rice porridge for us, and while we're eating, Baba comes out of Bao-bao's room dressed in a short-sleeved, white button-front shirt and black trousers. I watch with enormous relief as he plugs in an electric razor, shaves, and combs back his hair. He's mostly steady on his feet. I try to catch Mama's eye to see if she notices the change in him, but she stays focused on her bowl.

My flash of optimism drains out of me as I look between the two of them. Mama has always seemed so mindful of Baba in the times I've seen them on the holidays—asking him to taste this or that as she was cooking, telling him to put a scarf on. And he was always agreeable to her plans. They got along well. But now they seem like two strangers occupying the same space.

"Baba. Eat something!" I ladle up the porridge for him and hold it toward him.

He shakes his head and perches on the edge of the bed like he's waiting for something. His hands are folded in his lap and after a moment they begin to tremble.

"Na, where's the baijiu?" he asks me.

Mama glances up at Baba, taking in the sheen of moisture on his forehead and the tight clasp of his hands as he tries to stop the shaking. She flicks her wrist at me to go ahead and get it. I dig out the bottle from my bag and hand it to Baba. After yesterday and last night, it's been drunk down to a third. Baba takes a long swig and closes his eyes, letting the alcohol take effect. After several moments he hands the bottle back to me.

"Put it away now," he says. "We have to go."

My eyes widen. "Where are we going?" I ask eagerly, pleased that we're getting out of the apartment, that we're going somewhere. Together.

He doesn't answer. Mama gets up and nosily chucks her bowl into the plastic tub for washing dishes. She finds a white blouse and pulls it on over her tank top.

"Come on," she says, picking up her purse. "We have to get your brother."

My mouth falls open in confusion, but in half a second I catch on to what she means. I don't know why I haven't wondered where Bao-bao's body is before now. Hospital, morgue, cemetery? I guess I had so many questions about his death that where he ended up was the least of them. Yeye and some old folks from the village are the only people I've known who've died. I don't know what happens to the dead in the city.

Outside, the morning sky is hazy, with the ball of sun in soft focus over the rows of apartment complexes. Except for a group of ladies doing tai-chi, the plaza of the Glorious Towers is empty as we cross the expanse of concrete. We're halfway across when a woman comes in through the front gates, her short boots echoing with each step.

I see that she's young, not much older than me, dressed as if she's just coming in from a night out. Her long hair is messy and loose, and heavy makeup is smudged around her eyes, but her lips are bare. The short black dress she wears is studded with metal grommets along the side, and the neckline hangs sharply off one shoulder, revealing a large red-orange tattoo blooming across her pale skin.

Her stride is languid and confident. I see her eyes drift over me, move off, and jump back, suddenly alert. Her mouth parts slightly and she gazes at me steadily with a look I can't decipher. Mama and Baba, with their heads bent, don't take any notice of her since she passes with a wide berth. But she is close enough that I can see that the flaring tattoo, which I thought was a flower, is actually a nine-tailed fox.

I glance back once more as we exit the gate, but Mama picks up the pace. We walk several blocks while the city begins to wake up. Soon Mama has no choice but to slow down because Baba is dragging behind, patches of sweat showing up on the back and under the arms of his shirt. We have to stop so he can mop his face and smoke a cigarette. Mama doesn't say anything, but her face is cramped, anxious and miserable, and I sense the intensity of her impatience.

The bus takes us to the north edge of the city, and we get off at Farewell Row. Mama charges ahead, but I look left and right at the hearses parked in the potholed street, at the funerary shops selling firecrackers, incense, and wreaths. In the windows of several shops, women hunch over tables, scissoring and pasting elaborate three-dimensional papercuts of everything from oxen and gold mountains to refrigerators, cars, and Gucci purses.

Baba's lips are trembling when we arrive at the small brown brick storefront of Feng's Crematorium. An exhaust pipe rises up through the roof near the back of the building, expelling plumes of smoke. I flinch, registering that Bao-bao has been burned up, transformed into dust and smoke. With Yeye, there was an elaborate procession through the village with music and wailing, seven days of rites, endless offerings and gatherings. I suppose we'll take Bao-bao to the village and do the same, only without the coffin.

Inside, a large desk claims the center of the room, with shelves on three walls holding urns of every shape and color with price cards propped against each one of them. Mama tells Mr. Feng, a tall man with thin lips, that she has come to pick up Bao-bao's ashes.

"You want to take them?" Mr. Feng's forehead crinkles up. "You should have told me beforehand. It's not customary. Parents aren't supposed to show respect to their child!"

Mama clutches her hands against her middle and dips her head, but her jaw is set stubbornly. "That may be so, but times are changing," she says quietly.

Mr. Feng shakes his head. "The unmarried sons are left with us and we take care of . . . burying the ashes." He seems awfully keen for Mama to leave Bao-bao here. I wonder if he has already *buried* him.

"We want to take him home!" Baba bellows, his voice booming off the walls of the small shop. He pivots to scan the urns, his eyebrows furrowed in a way that seems almost belligerent.

He moves toward a blue and green cloisonné urn with an intricate design of orange carp swimming among water lilies. An upraised white oval on the side marks space for an image of the deceased. Over his shoulder, I see the price card is marked 300 yuan. I expect him to move away, so when he picks up the urn and passes it to Mr. Feng, a strangled noise escapes me.

Three hundred yuan is almost a month's tuition at my school! My eyes dart to Mama. Her expression is stony, and I can't tell if she's appalled at the extravagance or if she's simply brooding over Bao-bao and just doesn't care.

While Mr. Feng is in the back, Baba searches his wallet for the money. He doesn't have enough and Mama has to dig into her bag for the rest. As I watch them count out the bills, I suddenly realize that with Bao-bao gone there will be no more private school tuition to pay, no more extra class fees, no more gifts for teachers. At least Mama and Baba's constant money worries will ease up now.

Of course Mama and Baba are not concerned about this. They only smooth out the bills and have them ready when Mr. Feng returns.

♦ ♦ ♦

When we get back to Glorious Towers, the young woman from earlier this morning passes through the stairwell door from the sublevel. She has changed her clothes, now wearing jeans and a fitted brown leather vest. A professional camera bag is slung on her shoulder and her hair is pulled back in a tight, high ponytail.

She hesitates in the doorway when she sees us approaching. Her eyes flick to each of us, lingering on me again so that I'm almost expecting her to speak to me. But instead, her gaze shifts to Bao-bao's urn cradled in Mama's arms. She moves aside and holds the door open for us with her head tilted forward in a way that seems solemn and reverential. I'm the last to go through, and as I pass, she lifts her head and draws her eyebrows up and back in acknowledgement of my blatant stare.

I have to look away to watch my footing on the steps in the dark stairwell. When I get to the bottom of the flight, I glance back up to the door. The woman is gone and the door is closing, but I already have it in my mind that maybe she knew Bao-bao.

5

After lunch, Mama goes to work for a few hours. Baba carries Bao-bao's urn to the bedroom and sets it on the desk with the lamp shining down on it. He comes back out for the beer he pressured Mama into buying on the way home, then retreats into the bedroom and shuts the door.

In the front room, I chew on my thumbnail, wondering about Baba's drinking. When he was home for the Spring Festival, he always drank a lot, but most of the men did because it was the holidays. He's been sober enough all morning, but with the alcohol he's taken to his room, I'm afraid it's just a matter of time before he has another episode like yesterday. *Take care of him*, Mama said, but I'm not sure what that really means. There is nothing to do but wait.

I take out my phone to finally text Gilbert. The girls at college tease me about Gilbert being my boyfriend, but I'm not really sure. When he and I are together, I feel a spark, a charge, *something* between us, but he's never acted on it other than to give my hair a playful yank when we pass each other on campus. Whether this is because our parents drummed a *no dating* rule into us, or because Gilbert is as shy as I am, I don't know. But in truth, I don't mind that nothing's happened yet, because it's reassuring to think he has as little experience with romance as I do.

The message window blinks at me to start typing, but I don't know what to say about what's happened. I hesitate for a long minute. Eventually, I just come out with it.

Bao-bao died.

I stare at the phone waiting for an answer, but I know that if Gilbert's in Willow Tree Village, reception at his house might be poor, and he may not get my message right away.

There's no reply, so I make myself useful by cleaning up, washing the dishes, then washing some clothes in the utility room down the hall. While I'm hanging the laundry up on the line strung across the front room of the apartment, my eye falls on a book in the stack of clutter in the corner. *Harvard Girl Liu Yiting: A Character Training Record.*

Baba's wet undershirt slips off the line as I reach for the book. The cover shows a girl proudly displaying her Harvard acceptance letter. Of course, I've heard of the book: one couple's detailed methods and techniques for helping their daughter *achieve her full academic potential!* The book is still famous even though it was written years ago

Mama's copy is well-thumbed. Several pages are dog-eared, and lines are highlighted in yellow. I can envision Mama, with her middle school education, underlining, highlighting, marking down important points to remember for Bao-bao's sake.

I feel like crying, but instead I rip the cover off the book, then rip it again in half and crush all the pieces into a ball.

When Bao-bao went to live with Mama and Baba, I turned my resentment to my school work. I studied and studied and studied, finishing middle school with the highest rank. I knew education was the best way out of the countryside, the best way to avoid menial labor. I wanted to go on to high school, then to university. After that anything was possible. Mama and Baba said it all the time to Bao-bao.

But high schools are costly, and there wasn't one in the village anyway. Mama and Baba's finances were stretched with Bao-bao's education and with the cost of living in the city. They talked about me *going out* to work in a factory.

I wanted to leave the village, live in a city. Everyone did. But not to work in a factory.

Now with the crumpled book cover in my hand, I suddenly remember all the money Mama and Baba won't be spending on Bao-bao anymore. It occurs to me that Baba and Mama might direct some of that money toward me now. It's a self-serving thought, I know, but my heart races, wondering what that would mean for my education, my future.

My phone dings and I jump as if I've been caught in some guilty act. I quickly stuff what's left of the book into the bottom of my bag.

Are you kidding?! The text is from Gilbert.

Me: *No.* I type out the big-eye-short-mouth emoticon.

Gilbert: *How?*

I hesitate, then type the horrible word. *Suicide.*

After I hit send, I instantly regret it, knowing Gilbert will probably tell his family and soon the whole village will know and Nainai, all alone out there, will be even more distressed. Maybe people will be sympathetic, or maybe they'll think our family is unlucky and avoid her, but they will certainly gossip about us.

I add, *Ma and Ba can't talk about it. Too sad.*

Gilbert: *Why?*

Me: *?? Bad score on gaokao.*

Gilbert: *@#!!4&*! Are you okay?*

No one has asked me this. And in truth, the question strikes me as wrong, misdirected, as if, because of the distance between Bao-bao and me over the years, I have no claim to anyone's sympathy. Shock is the only thing I can convey.

Me: *I can't believe it.*

I grope for something else to say, but nothing comes to mind. I don't want the conversation to end. This stuffy, cluttered room and Baba's closed door are too grim.

Gilbert: *Wanted to save face?*

Me: *I'm not sure what to think.*

Gilbert: *Depressed?*

Me: *I didn't know him at all.*

The conversation stalls because I can't express the feelings roiling inside me. How could Bao-bao have scored so poorly after everything our parents did to help him, all the money they spent on him, rather than on themselves or me? He could have tried harder, or at least tried again next year. He threw away everything they invested in him. And then he threw away his life.

It seems so wrong to be angry at my own dead brother, even selfish. But wasn't he selfish to kill himself and make our parents suffer so much? I chew on the idea of dialing up Gilbert to talk, but Baba is just in the next room, and talking about everything out loud seems even more overwhelming.

My phone dings again. Gilbert has sent me a link. *Tragic Consequences for Gaokao Takers.* I click on the article and read about two separate incidents of students who've killed themselves due to exam stress. *A disturbing pattern each year in June... Competitive job market . . . future prospects . . . entrance to a top university is the first step to upward mobility . . .*

Another link pops up from Gilbert. This one is a YouKu video. *Student Leaps to His Death from School Window.* The video is a classroom monitor showing the students at work at their desks. It's been edited to fade out everything except one boy in the front row who stares blankly ahead rather than poring over his books. Suddenly, he rises, takes three steps to the left, and throws himself out the window. I gasp and slap my hand over my mouth to smother my horror. The newscaster narrating the video rambles on about *enormous pressure*.

Pressure.

I always thought Bao-bao was the perfect high-achieving son who got all the attention, but I suppose Mama and Baba were always telling him what to do, pushing him to study, looking over his shoulder. I never considered how stressful the long hours of study and the intense competition must have been for him.

I picture him scrolling down to his score, falling back against the chair, despondent at having failed Mama and Baba. Did he sit there numbly like the boy in the video until he rose and swallowed the poison in a daze? Or did he jump up and pace his room, tearing at his hair, until the idea of eating the poison sprang into his head?

I chew my fingernails, wondering if there's a news article about his death. I consider searching, but I hear a tap on the door.

When I open it, a man wearing thick glasses and a button-down short-sleeve shirt is standing there.

"Who are you?" he asks.

I tell him my name.

"Ah, the daughter? You haven't come to live here, have you?"

People are always so nosy, but it's clear he knows my parents so I try to be polite. "Why are you asking?"

"I'm the rent collector. Is your ba or ma home?"

Baba is in the bedroom, of course, but he's probably drunk, and I don't want to wake him. "No," I lie. "They're working extra shifts. They'll be home tonight." I have no idea what time Mama will be home, so I add, "Late. Or tomorrow." I hope Mama doesn't go to work on Sunday.

The rent collector glances at Bao-bao's door and purses his lips. Baba's snoring is loud through the thin walls. I hear the cot creaking as he shifts.

"My brother," I say stupidly.

The rent collector gives me a look that is both withering and pitying. He shakes his head slightly. "I know what happened to your brother."

I bite my lip, embarrassed I've been caught in a lie. "Baba's sick. It won't do any good to talk to him now," I say.

"Sick?" He eyes me in a questioning, doubtful way that infuriates me, but I don't show it. I just want him to leave.

"Yang!" Baba roars out Mama's name from the other room. "Yang!"

"No, Baba, it's just me!" I call over my shoulder. I have the urge to slam the door in the rent collector's face.

"Yang!"

I bolt to the other room, hoping to calm him, but Baba is already lumbering up to the door. "Who's out there? Who're you talking to?"

"It's no one. I'll—"

"It's me, Zhang Chu!"

I twist around and give the rent collector a murderous look.

Baba pushes past me, still in his good clothes, but they're wrinkled. "Rent's due already?"

Mr. Zhang nods. "Yes. And you're already two months behind."

Two months behind on the rent? My stomach plummets to my feet.

I edge in to stand beside Baba. Creases from sleep are etched on his face. He looks dumbfounded by this news and he pats at his pockets as if he's searching for his wallet. I know he doesn't have any money. He spent it all on Bao-bao's urn.

His head swivels, scanning the room, as if he's trying to find something to focus on. "My wallet . . . Na, have you seen . . ." He staggers. I grab his arm and try to lead him over to the bed.

"No!" Baba jerks his arm out of my grasp; his long pinky nail scratches my cheek. I gasp and reach up to touch the wound, but Baba doesn't notice because he is yelling.

"I have to get this bastard his money!" He shambles across the room, swatting aside the damp clothes on the line. He grabs the basket and begins to toss out the laundry I haven't hung up yet. It's as if he doesn't notice that they're wet. He doesn't know what he's doing.

"Baba!" I'm scared and frozen in place. My mind scrambles to the baijiu hidden in my bag.

"Have to get his money so he'll go away," Baba roars. "So he'll GET THE HELL OUT OF HERE!" He twists around and narrows his eyes at Mr. Zhang, utter disgust scrawled on his face. "After a day like this! Don't you have any kind of soul?"

Mr. Zhang's chin is pulled back. Baba's made him angry but he doesn't say anything.

"Mr. Zhang." I force myself to be polite and swallow my embarrassment for Baba, for lying. "My mama handles all the money. I would really appreciate it if you'd come back tomorrow." I'm desperate to get him to leave. I almost consider playing on his sympathy about Bao-bao, but that would shame us and Baba would probably fly apart.

Mr. Zhang's mouth is small and tight. I see him eyeing the scratch on my face. I cover it with my hand.

"Tell your ma to come to my office first thing tomorrow," he says.

I shut the door after he leaves. Baba is jerking down the wet clothes and slapping them into the basket and muttering, "Where's my wallet, where's my . . . Bao-bao." He doubles over and heaves. Nothing comes out at first, but he heaves again and thin vomit shoots from his mouth into the basket of wet clothes.

"Baba!" I cry out. I grab the plastic dishpan and thrust it under him. He retches and retches. The sour smell has me gagging.

The door opens and it's Mama, carrying several empty cardboard boxes. She drops the boxes and darts over to take the dishpan from me. I scuttle over to a stool and press one hand over my mouth and the other hand against my seizing gut, trying not to throw up myself.

My eyes are squeezed tightly shut, but I can hear that Baba's retching has slowed. He's sobbing, moaning, "Bao-bao, my boy, my boy, my boy is gone!" Mama says nothing.

I open my eyes and see tears running down Mama's cheeks. Their anguish kills me. There is nothing more frightening than to see one's parents cry.

6

I press a washcloth to the scratch on my cheek to stanch the thin line of bleeding while Mama tries to calm Baba, first scolding him for how he's acting, then telling him to settle down and go back to bed. Her voice is soft but flat, and she glances at me as she searches out the baijiu. Her look of weary trepidation makes me turn away and toss the washcloth into the basket of newly-soiled laundry.

The scratch doesn't hurt. I know Baba didn't mean to do it, and I don't want her to fret about one more thing. My cheek is still damp from the wet cloth and I resist the urge to swipe at it with the back of my hand until she goes into the other room.

The clothes Baba pulled down are all over the place, but I have to take care of the dishpan and the laundry basket first. I cover them with a towel before I carry them out of the apartment.

In the laundry room, I rinse the dishpan and clothes in the sink, then throw the clothes into the washer for another short cycle. As I lean against the machine to wait for them, I can't help but wish I was back at college with my roommates, chucking sunflower seeds at Xiaowen as she lip-syncs songs playing on her phone, or even sitting in the classroom as the teacher lectures about steam turbine generators and air quality control systems.

Hard to believe I was there just two days ago, happy to be done with my first year of college. Linfen Coal Economic Vocational High School and College isn't anyone's dream school, and coal production technology would never have been my first career choice, but I've been content there because it's certainly better than toiling away in a factory.

It was Gilbert who saved me from the factory when I was fifteen. During the Spring Festival of my last year of middle school, when our parents were visiting each other, talk came up about our futures. I was stuffed in my coat, lined up with Nainai, Bao-bao, and our parents on Gilbert's family's couch.

Gilbert's ma and ba perched on stools, sipping tea while Baba patted Bao-bao's leg and reported on Bao-bao's first year in Taiyuan with them. Then Gilbert's ma, with her tight curls of permed hair wobbling, jabbered about how she wished Gilbert, who was enrolled in vocational high school in Linfen, found more time to practice English, called home more, and ate more vegetables so he wouldn't get so many stomachaches. Gilbert sat at the table out of his ma's sightline. He took his glasses off, rubbed his face, and rolled his eyes with exaggerated exasperation, trying to make me smile.

When Baba said he was going to help me find a position in a factory, Gilbert dropped his funny expression. He pushed his glasses back on and raised his eyebrows at me. I blinked back grimly. Baba and Mama had already told me this several times on the phone over the previous year.

Gilbert pulled a face that said, *Ugh!*

I couldn't help but let out a laugh—at his look, not about working in the factory, which seemed like a life sentence.

All the parents looked at me. I immediately clamped my lips together and rearranged my expression.

Gilbert's ma turned to Mama. "Why are you sending Na to work? She's smart, the highest ranking in her class, isn't she? Gilbert wouldn't have passed his English for the high school entrance exam if she hadn't helped him, and she was two years younger! She's going to score well on the entrance exam! Much better than Gilbert did."

My pulse quickened. I looked down, feigning modesty, although inside I was gloating that she was bragging about me.

"Really, she's like that girl in the book, *Anne of Green Gables*. Competitive about her grades!" Gilbert said. I sniffed out a laugh. Our textbooks in English class had only featured excerpts focusing on Anne's determination to make the best scores. I had given Gilbert his nickname after Anne's rival. The name stuck even though he really wasn't that studious. Gilbert had found a complete copy of the novel in Linfen earlier in the year and sent it to me. I found out that Anne is also a high-spirited, imaginative girl who wants to be a writer and gets into all kinds of trouble. In the end she wins a scholarship, but passes it up to stay home and help out her family when her father dies.

Mama sighed, and Baba leaned forward in his seat to flick his ashes into the ashtray on the table. This was his cue to complain about money, how much everything cost—everything I had heard from them so often. I tuned it out.

"But the fees for some of the vocational schools are really low." Gilbert got up from his chair and went around to the other side of the table to perch on the edge of it. He had shot up in the last year, taller than both our fathers. "Much less than regular high schools, only about 350 yuan. And a person can continue straight into the technical college after high school. That's what I plan to do."

Baba leaned back in his chair, crossed his legs, and began joggling his socked foot. "Well, our expenses are already so overloaded." He directed his comments to Gilbert's ma and ba, ignoring Gilbert. "And with college coming up for Bao-bao in a few more years, Na's *going out* will really help the family." He and Mama both gave me regretful smiles that pulled down the corners of their mouths. "You want to help out the family, eh Na? You're a good girl, eh?"

It was my turn to receive a couple of pats on the leg from Ba. I stiffened, my jaw tensing to hold in the sourness churning in me.

"Na can get a more skilled technical position if she goes to a high school like Coal Economic," Gilbert said. My eyebrows shot up and I couldn't help but grin. He was being almost rude by speaking up to my parents, but I was grateful to him for doing it when I couldn't.

Baba waggled his head irritably and reached forward to stub out his cigarette. "By the time she finished all that school, then it would be time for her to get married, and then poof, she's gone from us. *Having a daughter is like spilled water.*"

Everyone laughed except Gilbert and me, and Bao-bao who raised an eyebrow my way.

"Ah! It's not like that anymore!" Gilbert's ma clicked her tongue. "The children now all go away anyway and live where they have to for the best job. And you have two children when so many people have just one. If you can afford to do well by this one too, you should do it. Besides, Huan will be there to help her out." She cocked her head, pointed her elbow out toward Gilbert, and smiled meaningfully. "Maybe something will grow from that. If Na marries someone from Willow Tree, she'll always come home here."

I turned flame red and Mama was quick to state, "No dating! They're too young to think about that!" But she covered her smile with her hand and Baba's eyebrows arched speculatively as his eyes danced from Gilbert to me.

Somehow, Mama convinced Baba that they could afford it. I was thrilled to go to Linfen, even though it was an industrial city—much dirtier than living in the countryside, but slightly less provincial. At least the little I saw of it, since the school was on the outskirts and we didn't leave campus often.

The high school had a lot of rules. No dating, a regimented schedule, a strict curfew. But the classes weren't too hard and I didn't have to work as much as students in an academic school. I spent my free time with my roommates or reading. I also kept my English language workbooks from middle school under my mattress and flipped through them sometimes, quietly scribbling vocabulary and mouthing the words for practice. The college level gave us a little more freedom, but mostly I've kept on with much the same routine. Only two days gone from all that, and I'm already longing to get back to my old normal life.

Now in the washroom, the laundry is done. I pile the wet clothes in the basket and go back to our apartment. Baba has quieted down, and Mama comes out of the bedroom as I start to hang up the rinsed-out clothes. Her hair is wild and her shoulders, mouth, and eyes slump downward so heavily I can almost see the burden of grief sitting on her. She stumbles over to the bed to sit beside me and presses her hands against her cheeks.

"Mama, lie down," I say. "I'll make us something to eat."

She shakes her head, gets up and begins to collect the rest of the laundry that Baba threw around.

"Mama! Let me do that!" I rush over and grab the clothes out of her hand. She stands in the center of the room looking at the mess that Baba made. Her gaze lands on the boxes she's brought in.

"Na," she says, "we're moving downstairs. I need you to help pack up the apartment tomorrow."

"Downstairs? But you're already in the basement!"

"There's another sublevel below this one. The rooms are even cheaper there."

Down farther below ground. For a moment I'm speechless, with a smothering sensation in my chest. Cheaper, smaller, darker? I'm sick that they have to live like this. I don't want to mention Mr. Zhang now, but I'm afraid not to. "Mama, the rent collector was here."

"I know. I saw him in the lobby."

"He said you're two months late. Will he let you move when you owe so much already?"

"I gave him some money. We're okay for now. At least with the rent. But we have some other debts." The muscles at her jaw twitch, then tighten as if she's trying to compose herself. She grabs my hand and pulls me over to sit on the bed. "Listen, Na . . ." She trails off when she notices the scratch on my face, and she runs her finger under it. "What's this?"

"Nothing. It was an accident. When Baba . . . got sick."

"Baba did this?" A look of horror comes over her.

"Mama, it's nothing! You saw how he was. I was just trying to get him to sit, and he . . . stumbled. He has that long pinky nail. It was an accident." I'm blathering, but I just want her to stop worrying.

Her hand slides off my cheek. "An accident." The distant, hollow Mama is back.

"Mama." I grip her forearm and shake it gently. "What were you going to tell me?"

She blinks several times before she focuses on me again. "Baba has to go home. To Willow Tree. He's not able to work like this. You have to take him home. I'll finish moving us down to the new apartment while you're gone. After you get Baba settled, then you have to come back here. We'll get you a position. Na, with the debts and Baba not working, we need you to help out now."

"Of course," I say, nodding vigorously. I want to help all I can. "If I take Baba this week and come back right away, I can start looking for something. I'll have six or seven weeks to work before school starts up."

Mama cocks her head and looks at me for a long moment with the saddest expression. "No, Na." She shakes her head mournfully. "There's no more school for you."

7

When Mama tells me that I'm not going back to school, that I have to go to work, I swallow the news like bitter medicine. Parents make the decisions, and we must go along with them. They allowed me to go to high school and one year of college, but now I'm needed to ease their burden. It's another unexpected blow, but of course I can't argue, or protest, or even try to come up with other alternatives. Not after everything that's happened.

We clean up the apartment in silence, both us working in sort of a daze. As I make dinner, eat, and try to sleep, the words *No more school for you* rise up like a lump in my throat again and again, but I gulp them down. My self-pity is blunted by the image of Baba sick and raging, the picture of him cradling Bao-bao, and the sight of Mama moving around like a dreamwalker during the day and tossing around sleepless at night. The situation is tenuous here and my own disappointment is paltry in comparison.

On Sunday, Mama gets Baba installed in the front room drinking tea so I can start packing up Bao-bao's things. She is going to work again, another extra shift, although I try to talk her out of it.

"I need to work!" she snaps at me. Her hands fly to her temple and she squeezes her eyes shut. "The money . . ." she starts to explain, shifting to a softer, placating tone, but I know that she must be trying to bury herself in work. She takes another deep breath and collects her purse. "When you start work, I'll cut back," she promises.

She leaves, and I'm left with Baba and the awful feeling of resignation. Baba is sitting up in the bed with his legs stretched out and his eyes closed. I can tell he's just dozing because his hands are wrapped around his jar of tea. My hand goes up to my cheek where he scratched me. I can barely feel the line of it.

I take two of the boxes Mama brought in last night and enter Bao-bao's room. His urn is on the desk. The golden edging that snakes between the colored enamel glints in the circle of lamplight, and the white oval where Bao-bao's photo should be seems to follow me like a great unblinking eye.

I turn my back to it and begin to sort the textbooks and notebooks. Mama mentioned selling them, but I want to keep some of them for myself, especially the history and English language ones. Perhaps in the evenings after my workday, I'll have time to study and read. There won't be much room in the second sublevel apartment Mama showed me last night, so I'll have to lug some of them to Willow Tree Village. I work rapidly to put them into the boxes. I avoid looking at the urn, but even so, I sense its presence. For a moment I consider moving it out to the front room, but I don't want to do anything that might disrupt Baba's mellow mood.

The stuff on the wall comes down next. The school certificates, the calendar, posters. On the wall near the low iron footrail of the bed, there's a sheet of red paper with a quote in English.

I untack it and hold it closer to the lamp. *Freedom is a strange thing. Once you've experienced it, it remains in your heart, and no one can take it away. —Ai Weiwei*

Ai Weiwei is a famous artist and political activist. I don't know much about him other than that he was one of the primary designers of the Bird's Nest Olympic Stadium and has been in trouble for being critical of the government. I'm surprised to see the quote here on Bao-bao's wall. Although Bao-bao was interested in art once, I always thought he quit after middle school. The words are hand-painted in yellow, the streaks of the brush visible like slashes. Bao-bao must have painted it himself, as if the line held a powerful meaning for him.

It remains in your heart, and no one can take it away. The statement is hopeful and defiant. I try to imagine Bao-bao lying on his bed, staring at the words, trying to draw strength from them.

But the boy I see is hopeless and sad. Someone who has given up. I didn't know the struggle he was going through, and I don't understand how he scored so poorly on the test, but the shame of it, of failing our parents, anyone can understand that. Even if his reaction still seems staggeringly drastic.

I slip the little poster between two notebooks and then start to strip the bed. On an impulse, I bend back the thin mattress, thinking of where I keep my English notebooks and workbooks at school.

My heart skips a beat when I see a folder lying on the grid of wire that holds the mattress. I pull it out, let the mattress flop back into place, and sink down on the rumpled sheets. As soon as I open the folder, I inhale sharply. Inside is an image of a proud, pointy-nosed fox with nine tails swishing out behind him in fiery shades of red-orange, tipped in white. I've seen it before. The girl in the courtyard had this exact image tattooed on her shoulder.

I pick up the sheet to hold it closer to the light and find that there's another drawing in the folder. This one's a portrait, a headshot done in pencil. Right away, I recognize the girl in the courtyard. The lift of her chin and set of her open mouth are drawn so deftly, there's no mistake. Her hair flows from her face like rays of the sun. Did Bao-bao draw these? I wonder who she is. Clearly, she meant something to him. Was she his girlfriend? But he was only seventeen, and I would guess she's a few years older than me, probably in her twenties.

I plop down on the bed, examining the portrait. That Bao-bao would even know an older girl this striking, with a tattoo, fractures my mind. All these years, Mama never mentioned Bao-bao's friends, and the way she explained his schedule, it seemed that he didn't have time for any. Obviously, she didn't know about this girl, since she paid no attention to her when we passed her in the courtyard and the lobby.

And when did Bao-bao find time for drawing? These illustrations are so well done, so beautifully styled, they suggest that Bao-bao probably kept drawing all through high school. When we were left behind together in Willow Tree, he drew trees, animals, even insects. Even back then I was struck by his talent. Nainai and I admired his drawings until she had to say, *Now get back to your homework.* Sometimes when Bao-bao balked at having to study I'd tell him I would write a story while he did his work, and then he could draw the pictures for the story when I was finished.

I smile, remembering how that always worked.

◆ ◆ ◆

Mr. Hu comes to stay with Baba so I can start to clean the new apartment and move some things. I go down alone with a broom, a dustpan, and the trash can. Mama has given me a key. I let myself in and yank on the string attached to the caged bulb in the center of the low ceiling.

The room is dank, smelling of dead mice, and the previous tenant has left the floor littered with newspapers, rags, and cigarette butts. I sweep, trying not to let the walls close in on me, trying not to sink into despair about my shrinking future here in this room. I keep the broom swishing and speed through the cleaning, desperate to get out of here.

Twenty minutes later I'm out in the passageway, locking the door. I hear the flap of slippers, and I squint in the low light to see someone in a red tank top and shorts stop at the end of the hall, letting herself into an apartment. It's the girl from the courtyard.

I dash back upstairs, nod at Mr. Hu, and grab a box of Bao-bao's textbooks. The drawings in the folder I found are tucked in with the books. Baba's awake and staring at the ceiling. He doesn't even look my way when I leave.

Downstairs, I put the books in the new room, remove the folder with Bao-bao's drawings, and carry them to the girl's apartment. I knock. She swings the door open, holding a phone to her ear. Her brows lift and I know she recognizes me, but she stays on the phone.

A tinny voice screeches through the line, "*If you're not there I will come over and pick you up!*"

"Okay, Ma, okay," the girl answers, "I'll meet you. I'll see you there." She clicks off and gazes at me expectantly.

I open the folder and show her the portrait. "Is this you?" I ask.

She takes it. Her face seems to melt as she examines it for several moments before she looks back to me with a pained expression. "I'm Min. You're Bao-bao's sister?"

I nod. "Na." She opens the door and gestures at me to come in. I see her room is even smaller than ours down the hall, but it has the same low ceiling and naked bulb overhead. Strings of colored lights are draped over the shelves and across the room. A desk with a laptop on it is crammed against the bed, and shelves overloaded with clothes and books are fastened to almost all the wall space.

"You look just like him." Her two forefingers trace a heart in the air, indicating the shape of the face Bao-bao and I shared.

"How did you know him?" I ask.

"He used to come to the internet café I go to."

I blink back my surprise. "Internet café? Why didn't he just use the internet at school?"

"He hung out there often. Started coming with his basketball friends to play *League of Legends*. Then he started coming over more and more—skipping classes!" She shakes her head like he was a silly kid, so I know there was no romantic interest. At least on her part.

"I go to the café to work." She flips her hand toward her laptop and the shelf over the desk with camera equipment. "The internet is so slow down here. He always wanted to see the photos I was working on. After we talked about what we would want if we ever got tattoos, he drew this." She holds up the illustration of the nine-tailed fox against the twin image tattooed on her shoulder. "I liked it so much, I actually got it done."

I'm speechless, picturing this Bao-bao. I've only ever heard about how Bao-bao was studying, choosing his education track, practicing English. This guy who played basketball and video games, designed tattoos, skipped classes, I've never known. And our parents? Did they know?

"I'm sorry about what happened," Min says. She pushes the desk's rolling stool at me.

I nod dumbly and move to sit down, wanting to ask her more, but it's almost too much to take in. No wonder he scored so poorly on the gaokao.

"They must be so devastated," Min says. "I heard it was rat poison. I just don't . . ." She trails off with a doubtful curl to her lip. "I can't believe it," she murmurs. They're the same words I've said to myself dozens of times, but coming from her they seem to carry more weight. She knew Bao-bao, whereas I did not.

"Was he unhappy?" I ask.

She smooths the black comforter covering her bed and sits down, the folder open to the portrait beside her. "I didn't see that he was."

"But with all the pressure of the gaokao? My parents?"

She hikes her shoulder in an uncertain shrug. "He didn't let it bother him so much. He seemed very casual about the bad grades. Your parents berated him and nagged him, but somehow he could just let it roll off."

"I never knew about any of that." I'm stunned by what she is saying. "Mama never said."

"For a while, he was practically addicted to video games. It got to where he would hardly even stop to talk to me when he got up to get a Red Bull or snacks. Your baba came there last year and dragged him home. But he didn't stop coming even after your baba tried to keep him from it. He said they had you. That you could be their *little emperor* for a while."

I'm taken aback. Bao-bao talked about me, thought about me? And the remark seems to have a tinge of contempt, resentment. But not at me, surely. I know about resentment, and Bao-bao certainly had no reason to envy me.

All this is too much swimming in my head. I thank Min for talking to me, tell her I have to go, and head back upstairs.

8

After Mr. Hu leaves I move a few more boxes and get Baba some lunch. All the while my mind is on Bao-bao, this rebellious Bao-bao, the one who had to be dragged away from the internet café. I just can't believe that Mama never let on about any of it. It rankles that she never told me. I don't know why she didn't, but I know I can't ask her now.

My curiosity to know more gets the better of me, and as soon as Baba falls asleep after lunch, I slip back down to Min's.

"I have to meet my ma at the park," she tells me when she answers the door. She's now dressed in a pencil skirt, flats, and navy boat-neck shirt as if she's going to work in an office. Her tattoo is completely covered. "Come over tomorrow night?"

"I can't." Her friendliness is a balm to the last grim days, and I'm disappointed that I can't go. "I'm taking my baba home to our village tomorrow afternoon."

"Walk to the park with me, then. It's not far. You can turn around when we get there, be back in thirty or forty minutes."

I want to go but I dither, anxious about Baba. He did have several gulps of baijiu just before he moved back to the bedroom and fell asleep, and I did leave the bottle on the desk beside him, adding some water to it like Mama instructed.

The impulse to leave the basement overcomes me, so I agree.

We proceed along the poorly-lit corridor, surface up in the lobby and step outside. The air is hot and thick with the ever-present fug of the city, but it comes as a relief.

The courtyard is buzzing with hovering parents and children pedaling their tricycles and scooters. It's almost festive with the voices rising above the noise from the highway overpasses. Because it's Sunday, many of the factories are closed and there's much less traffic thrumming overhead.

Min walks at a brisk pace even though she's wearing heels. I thought I wanted to ask about Bao-bao, but at the moment, it's like I've shed a great heaviness, and I can't bear to bring up anything sad.

We don't talk for several blocks. I have to work to keep up with her. Her camera bag hangs across her shoulders and bounces on her hip. Her hair is smoothed and pulled back tightly. The eyeliner she wears is blue but otherwise, her appearance is professional, almost conservative.

"Have you ever been to the Marriage Market?" Min asks.

I shake my head.

"Got a boyfriend?"

I shrug. There's Gilbert, but not really.

She raises her eyebrows at my vague answer but doesn't pry any further. "My ma goes to the Marriage Market almost every week to look for my perfect match. She hounds me to go with her, constantly after me to get married. *Are you dating? Do you have a boyfriend? When are you going to bring someone home?* She started it all up as soon as I finished college." She snorts in annoyance. "Never wanted me to have anything to do with boys while I was in school, then expects me to get married the moment I graduate."

"You haven't met anyone yet?"

"Not at the Marriage Market! I'll walk around with her, looking at the profiles, getting drilled by parents with questions. *How old are you?* That's always the first question. *What's your position, how much money do you make?* I hate it! There's no way I'm going to pick someone based on their stats—how much money they make, their apartment, their car."

"But you go?" A mother's will is always strong, but Min seems so different than the girls I go to school with.

"Yes, I go." She bows her head, miming the attitude of a good daughter. "But only a couple times a year. Enough to keep her somewhat satisfied. And actually, today, I'm going because of a project I'm working on." She pats her camera bag.

"You're a photographer?" I've never met anyone who did that for a living. It certainly isn't a track of study at Linfen Coal Economic College.

"Yes."

"You make money doing that?"

She laughs. "Yes. I do a lot of pre-wedding photos, but I also do a lot of commercial work, styling for photo shoots and some other things. I'm working on an art installation and video now. It might not make me any money, but it should help with my business. My parents are very upset that I quit my communications job last year."

Her confidence isn't something I'm used to and I wonder what communications work entails. I want to ask her, but we've reached the park. The wide, paved path is crowded with old people and strolling couples. Hawkers run battery-operated toys and spinning tops right in the path of children and parents, driving the foot traffic into the grass despite the signs that order people to stay off.

Farther down the winding path, after we pass under an ornamental bridge, the crowd really thickens. Open umbrellas of every color are lined up on the ground on both sides of the walkway, each one with a single sheet of paper stuck on them. More sheets, some encased in plastic sleeves, hang off fencing and are laid out on the benches or along stone walls.

Min stops and pulls out her camera. I squint over the heads to read one of the sheets.

Male Taiyuan resident
Born 1994
Height: 175cm
Profession: Accounting
Income: 7,500/mo.
Honest, doesn't drink or gamble
Apartment: Owns
Looking for Taiyuan female with good temperament,
at least 165cm

"Those are stat sheets," Min explains as she clicks on a lens. "Everything that matters about your future spouse." She lifts the camera and begins to take photos of the crowd.

While she works, I study other profiles. Some of them are handwritten, others are printed like professional resumes. Some of them feature photos of the intended, but hardly any of them talk about personality or interests. I wonder how many people have really found their true match at this market.

The crowd shifts around me slowly. People are squinting at the stat sheets, taking notes, having urgent conversations. It's almost as if they're bargaining at the wet market over the quality and price of pork or mutton. I notice that almost every-one here is middle-aged or older. I nudge Min. "Where are all the young people?"

She sniffs out a laugh. "It's mostly the parents here, looking for their kids' spouses. The kids probably don't even know that their parents are out here trying to set them up."

I pull out my phone and snap a photo of a line of stat sheets strung between two trees. I text it to Gilbert, knowing he'll be amused.

Min asks, "How old are you?"

"Nineteen."

"Ah! Prime age! You'd better watch out. They'll be after you." She aims the camera and begins to photograph two men showing each other photos on their phone. "And you go to vocational college? No aspiration for a PhD?"

I shrug. I did have aspirations, although I never imagined anything as grand as a PhD. "I don't know if I'll be going back to college. After I take my baba home, I may have to go to work to help my family." I don't know why I say *may have to*, because I know it's already decided.

Min gives me a sympathetic look. "Well, if it makes you feel any better, my mama tells me the All-China Women's Fed-eration says, *Pretty girls don't need a lot of education to marry into a rich or powerful family.* And, *By the time you finish your MA or PhD, you're already old, like yellow pearls.*" I know she's being sar-castic because she makes a face.

"There you are!" A woman in a mushroom-shaped sun hat barrels toward us, pushing through the crush of parents. "Why are you pulling that ugly face? Stop it!" I assume it's Min's ma. There's a lanyard around her neck with a large clear plastic sleeve. On the slip of paper inside, I see Min's stats. "What are you doing with that camera? Put it away! And where's your hat? Your face is going to get tanned."

Min lets her mother's berating comments pass over her. Although she lowers the camera, she doesn't put it in the bag. "Ma, this is Na."

Min's ma notices me for the first time. She scrutinizes me. "How old are you?"

Min chuckles. Her ma throws her a look of annoyance before turning back to me.

After I tell her my age, she spins back to Min. "See! Already looking, and just nineteen. She has good sense! Why didn't you have the good sense to start earlier? You're twenty-six! Already almost *leftovers*!" She pulls a book out of her purse and pushes it at Min.

Min and I both look at the title. *You Should Marry Before You're Thirty*.

Min gives a little shake of her head and closes her eyes briefly as if trying to summon up more patience.

"Put that in your bag and read it at home," her ma says. "You need to get serious about this, right now. No man will want you once you're past childbearing age!"

Min closes her eyes for another moment, her lips drawn out in a tight line. I find myself expecting her to make a joke or sarcastic comment, but her ma tears the lanyard from around her own neck, slips it over Min's head, and tries to take the camera off of her. Min places her hand firmly on the strap until her ma releases it. Only after that does she stuff the book inside her bag.

"You want to come with us?" Min asks me.

"No!" Min's ma says firmly. "We have to get serious. No good to have another girl around!" She pushes Min toward the crowd, instructing her to stay close, to smile, to be polite.

Min twists around and raises a hand to wave at me. "Come see me again when you get back from your village."

I wave back and try to inch my way out of the crush. People, parents are beginning to examine me. One woman plants herself in my path and puts her face right up to mine. "How old are you?" she demands.

I duck my head and swiftly exit the park.

9

The next afternoon, Baba and I are on the bus to Willow Tree Village. Bao-bao's urn is in his lap, the gold strips between the enamel inlay glinting in the sun that streams through the window. Despite the heat, Baba is wearing a jacket—and tucked inside it is an old soda bottle filled with tea and baijiu, which he nips from occasionally.

Before we left the apartment, he and Mama argued about whether Bao-bao's urn should stay in Taiyuan or go to the village. Their voices were wheedling at first but rapidly grew heated, until Baba hissed that if Bao-bao stayed with Mama, he'd be left alone in the apartment all day while she and I went to work. Mama fell silent after that, with a muscle twitching at her jawline, as if she wanted to say more but knew that what Baba said was true. Baba calmed down then and promised to bring him back to her when he got better. I knew then that there'd be no funeral service for Bao-bao. *Parents aren't supposed to show respect to their child*, the cremation clerk said.

On the bus, Baba murmurs to the urn every now and then until he finally moves his unfocused eyes in my direction. "So you got a position?"

I make a noise of assent and look down at my hands, my

insides withering. Just this morning I went to the scrap metal plant with Mama, and her boss said he would have a place in the sorting room on the night shift in about two weeks.

Mama was hoping he'd give me a better position, something more in line with what I've learned at school. But coal and scrap metal have little in common, and the boss said sorting was all he could offer right now. Mama says I can look for something better later in the year once we catch up on our debts, but it's best to have something set for when I return from Willow Tree. At least I have two weeks to get used to the idea of working in the plant.

"Good." Baba's head tilts back against the seat. "You went to the high school, and I thought that was more than enough, but your mama, she said it wouldn't hurt to let you keep going to the college as long as we could afford it. Now it's time to go to work."

He turns to look out the window, to the flat, barren landscape we speed past with the occasional dilapidated buildings near the highway.

I turn away, trying not to think about the future, trying to suppress the flare of irritation at his tone, but Baba rambles on.

"We've spent too much money on school for your brother." His hand slips inside his jacket to bring out the baijiu-laced tea. He unscrews the lid and drinks deeply. "Better to work. You're almost twenty. Soon you'll find a boyfriend, get married."

My phone pings.

Marriage market? It's Gilbert, responding to the photo I sent him yesterday. He adds the frightened face emoji.

Baba glances at the phone. I quickly tuck it under my leg before he sees the text. "Baba, do you want to put that"—I gesture to the urn—"between us?"

Baba shakes his head. He clamps the urn between his knees, placing his free hand on it protectively.

I close my eyes and pretend I'm going to sleep. At least in Willow Tree, Nainai will be around to help with Baba. And Gilbert will be there, getting ready to start his new job as a mining operations associate in a neighboring township. I hope that he has time to see me. I'm sorry we missed our long bus ride home from college, the last one we would have had together.

Soft snores rattle from Baba's throat. He's fallen asleep against the window.

I pull out my phone and scroll back to the messages Gilbert sent me with links about students taking their own lives. I don't want to see the video of the boy jumping out the window again, but I type in another search with similar keywords.

I scroll through a list of articles once it finally loads. I click on one that mentions depression in the title. It's written by a psychiatrist who talks about the role of depression and anxiety in suicide. It quotes a young woman whose cousin killed herself: *I would visit her sometimes but I didn't know she was so unhappy. I knew she had worries about money, her in-laws—like we all do—but she had a house, a husband. Sometimes she seemed quiet, but everyone is so busy, no one ever stops to consider if their feelings are normal. I know they call it depression now, but no one out here likes to talk about that kind of thing.*

The article goes on to stress that depression is a mental illness that can show itself in many ways, including by driving people to self-destructive behavior. It says that people suffering from depression may not have any specific reason for feeling hopeless, but that outside circumstances can exacerbate their illness.

Bao-bao and I haven't talked much these last several years. For the two weeks in February during the Spring Festival, if he wasn't studying or sleeping in our room, he had his face glued to his phone or to the TV. Although Mama and Baba would chatter to anyone who stopped by to visit about his schedule and workload, he always ignored them, only greeting them when prompted. I thought he was spoiled and rude, but was he actually depressed?

And what Min told me about Bao-bao—skipping school, not caring about his rankings, flouting our parents' plans for him and doing what he wanted—does that fit in with depression?

I don't know. Like the woman who was interviewed for the article, I'm not used to thinking about this sort of thing. Mental illness. Back home it's considered embarrassing at best, shameful at worst.

The article says depression and anxiety are treatable. But I doubt my parents would have even noticed if Bao-bao was showing the symptoms of despair the article outlines. And even if they had, they would've had no idea how to help him. They would've simply urged him to pull himself together.

I study Baba while he sleeps. His forehead is creased and a sharp line cuts between his brows as if he's having a troubling dream. My hard feelings toward Bao-bao steal back in. He threw away all the opportunities our parents gave him, when I would have done anything for the same treatment. And now, what little I had is being taken away.

Baba mumbles beside me. "Bao-bao, Bao-bao. I'm sorry. I shouldn't have . . ."

Even in sleep Baba can't escape the guilt he must be carrying for pushing too hard. My frustration at him fades, replaced with pity.

10

When we get off the bus in Willow Tree, I hire a tricycle cart to transport the two large polyethylene bags full of Bao-bao's things to our yaodong at the edge of the village. I stashed some of the textbooks I wanted to keep in the apartment, but Mama couldn't bear to throw out Bao-bao's composition books and his clothes just yet. There wasn't room for them in the new apartment, so I lugged them here.

As the cart pulls ahead, I coax Baba to walk, wanting him to sober up as much as possible for Nainai. He drags along with his head down. We trudge down the paved main street, past the karaoke bar, the hair salon, and the internet café. Five or six streets make up the village center. It's grown to almost a town. A mix of old and new buildings house the shops, billiards halls, and hole-in-the-wall restaurants, everything coated in the brown silt of the mountains.

I'm sure Baba is hoping to avoid running into anyone we know, just like I am. Most of the residents are elderly people and children, along with a few men who still work the family lots. Everyone else has gone off to school or migrated to the cities to work. But with Baba holding Bao-bao's fancy urn, the children stop in the street to stare, while the shopkeepers peer out the windows and doors.

I steel myself for someone to say something, but we make it to the edge of the village without anyone grilling us. I wonder if Nainai or Gilbert has told anyone.

The hilly dirt lanes that spread out to the surrounding fields are lined with crumbling brown-brick houses and yaodongs, the common cave-shaped homes dug into the hillsides. Brick and wood enclose the front of each dwelling with a door and a single window, both framed within the arch. Several white tile houses have been built in and around the village, paid for by families' grown children who've gone away to work.

Nainai lives just outside the village in a two-room yaodong. As we approach the low brick wall enclosing her courtyard, I see the bags have been delivered. I catch sight of her silvery head and rail-thin frame bent over as she tries to drag one of the bags inside. It's way too heavy for her.

"Nainai! Stop!" I shout.

She squints out against the sun until she catches sight of us. Instantly she drops the handles of the bag and straightens up. Her tanned, lined face is instantly wet with tears. Seeing her cry makes my chest hurt, and Baba begins to choke out sobs. He holds out the urn as he walks up to Nainai, who is swiping away tears but doesn't make any noise. She pushes aside the quilt tacked over the open doorway and ushers us into the house.

The long, tunnel-shaped room is cool thanks to the surrounding packed earth. Nainai gestures to Baba to put Bao-bao's urn on the kang, the hip-high brick platform that takes up almost half the room. Bao-bao and I used to sleep, eat, and study on it until Nainai got a table and stools to place near the brick stove that's attached to the end of the kang.

Baba collapses onto one of the stools at the table, and Nainai stands behind him, squeezing his shoulder and shaking her head in grief. I hang back, not knowing what to do with myself. Light from the large window reflects off the whitewashed curved ceiling, with electrical cords crossing to the hanging bulbs and old boxy TV set in the corner of the kang near the stove. Newspapers and pictures from old calendars cover the wall, and several large frames with family photos hang near Nainai's padded chair. At the back of the room two large wardrobes section off the cot where Nainai sleeps.

It all looks exactly as it always has, cluttered yet tidy, but it's so strange to see Baba sitting at the table with his shoulders slumped, knowing he grew up here years before me and has now returned to be taken care of, indefinitely.

I hear a voice calling from outside. I spin around and push back the quilt to see Gilbert. He's wearing a button-down, short-sleeved shirt and has smoothed his bangs to the side. The wave of relief that washes over me is enormous. I beam at him as I let him in.

His brows flash up above his glasses as he grins back at me, but he quickly rearranges his face. When he sees Nainai and Baba, he nods at them gravely and mutters, "I hope you don't mind me stopping by. My grandma is so sorry for you. She wants to come to see you, and she sends you these eggs." He steps over to thrust a box toward Nainai.

Nainai takes it and sets it on the kang beside Bao-bao's urn. "Yes. Okay. I . . ." She averts her eyes and stammers, "Tell her okay. Come see us. I didn't know how to . . . couldn't talk about it . . ."

I swallow a lump in my throat as it sinks in that Nainai hasn't told anyone, not even Gilbert's grandma, who is probably her closest friend. She's been alone with her heartbreak, probably ashamed of the suicide, afraid of the gossip.

Baba stares dully at Gilbert.

"Have you eaten?" I ask Gilbert awkwardly, trying to drive some normalcy into the situation. It works and Nainai moves toward the stove.

"Yes, already eaten." He lowers his voice. "Can you come out for a little bit?"

I want to go, eager to be away from all the gloominess, but we've just gotten here. I start to say no, but Nainai flicks her hand for me to go ahead.

Gilbert mumbles his goodbye. Baba doesn't answer and we slip out the door.

When we're outside of the courtyard and a good distance down the path, Gilbert stops near a pile of large stones someone has collected for a wall. "Na! What the fuck! I don't know what to say."

"Nothing *to* say. It's terrible." I pick up some small pebbles and chuck them over the hillside.

He climbs up to the top of the pile and sits on the rocks. "How did it happen? I mean . . . that sounds macabre, I don't mean *how* exactly, but . . ."

"It's all right." So far, without anyone to talk to, I've been keeping everything bottled up. I'm glad to talk. "He swallowed rat poison." The words are still a shock to my ears. Such an unimaginable act. I just hope that it was painless, quick.

Gilbert shudders. "But . . . why? Was it really the gaokao?"

"Mama's neighbor said that's what the authorities determined. My parents don't talk about anything. They're too upset. I read those articles you sent. I guess it was like what happened to those kids—too much pressure, maybe combined with depression. My parents are devastated, blaming them-selves. Mama is silent, like an empty shell. She goes to work every chance she can. Baba, he's been drinking and sleeping all the time. He can't work. That's why I had to bring him back."

I worry that I'm revealing too much, telling him things I shouldn't, betraying my family by exposing their secrets, but I can't hold back.

"I just can't believe it!" Gilbert says.

"It's all so unreal. I don't believe Baba ever drank like this except at the Spring Festival. Maybe he did, I don't know. And Bao-bao." I shake my head. "It's like I never knew him. I thought he was such a hard-working student. But I met a friend of his, an older girl who told me Bao-bao skipped school to play video games. He designed a tattoo for this girl. A tattoo! That she has on her shoulder. It's like he was a completely different person than I thought."

Gilbert rests his arms on his knees, looking down at me from the rock pile, listening, sympathy all over his face as I unload everything that I haven't been able to talk about.

"He was giving our parents trouble. I didn't know that side of him at all. I keep thinking about the Bao-bao I knew from when we were kids. I used to have to trick him into doing his homework. But Mama always made it seem like he was the perfect student. She never let on that he was making things difficult or that he was unhappy." I heave a breath out my nose. We're all so absorbed with the narrow paths we've been assigned. Our parents with pushing Bao-bao to achieve at all costs. Me with my misguided resentment of him.

Tears are welling up in me, from regret, from Gilbert's compassion, from the stress of the last days. I grab another handful of gravel-sized rocks and throw them over hard, blinking the tears back. The rocks make a satisfying patter as they land and skitter downhill.

"Did he leave a note?"

I shake my head. No one mentioned a note, but all those composition books come to mind, and I begin to wonder.

"What's going to happen now?"

I shrug, my heart sinking. The only thing I know for sure is that I am not going back to school. I hate to say it out loud, but I know in just a couple of weeks when I go back to Taiyuan, it will become very real. "I have to go to work now. My parents need me to help out with some debts. School's over for me."

"What?" Gilbert shoots up and scuttles off the rocks. "No! Can't you find something just for the summer? You only have two more years to get your degree!"

"I've already got a job at my mom's plant. With Baba not working . . ."

"What about when he gets better? You still have more than six weeks before the term starts."

"I don't know," I say. "Mama must think it'll take longer than that. He's really not doing well. Besides, coal operations wasn't really what I wanted to study." I feel like I have to make excuses.

"So what?" Gilbert throws me a quizzical look. "You were glad to be there. You made good grades, and if you graduate you'll get a better job than sewing stuffed animals or working in a stall restaurant."

He's offended because he helped talk my parents into letting me go to school, and I'm offended because it's my future that everyone's deciding on.

"There's nothing I can do about it!" My voice is sharp with the strain in my throat and chest. "I have to help my family!"

Gilbert is sorry immediately. "Of course, of course. I know. We have to do what our parents tell us." His face softens, and he reaches for me and pulls me into a hug.

11

The questions I have about Bao-bao don't leave me, and late in the night after Baba and Nainai are fast asleep, I have a sudden impulse. I get out of my bedroll and lug the bag full of Bao-bao's books up onto the kang with me. In the yellowy light of the bulb hanging from the ceiling, I pull out all his exercise books and arrange them into stacks by school year.

When I have them neatly piled, I rest back on my folded knees. *Science, Chinese, Mathematics, History/Geography, English, Moral Education*—Bao-bao's handwriting is blocky and precise on the covers. I picture Bao-bao in his blue-and-white polyester school uniform, sitting at his desk among the rows of students, doing the compulsory eye exercises before settling down to work on his assignments.

My pulse, which just a few moments ago was racing with the idea of examining the books, has now slowed with the peculiar sensation that I am committing a trespass on Bao-bao, as if I'm snooping into his personal diary.

But these are just his school things, I tell myself. And it's just me, stewing with envy and resentment over his seven years of private schooling, who's imagining he would care.

I take one of his sixth-year workbooks and begin to turn

the pages, not really expecting to find a suicide note, but looking for clues about his frame of mind. The book is tidy, with page after page of class notes and assignments in Bao-bao's compact handwriting.

I rifle through all the sixth-year books, then move on to the next year, progressing through the stacks of middle school. They're all unremarkable except for the depth and number of his assignments, which causes an ache in my chest because the workload is so much more than I had at my village middle school.

I'm well into the ninth year when I come across a drawing of Chairman Mao sketched in the margins of Bao-bao's Moral Education notebook. I hold the book up to the light to get a better look at the drawing, which is small, done in pencil. With just a few strokes, the likeness of the stock image that often hangs in classrooms is unmistakable.

A few pages further, there's another drawing of Chairman Mao, larger this time with more detail and shading to his thick face and pointy collar. Bao-bao has gone off-model though, archly raising one of the man's eyebrows. The sketch is clearly of the famous leader, but I have the eerie sensation that it's Bao-bao looking up at me, wanting to know why I'm prying into his things.

I methodically keep flipping the pages, but no other sketches appear until the tenth-year workbooks. Within the first few pages, Bao-bao has drawn a teacher with her back to the class. I suppose she's his own teacher, and I smile, knowing he must've had to wait until she was writing on the board to avoid her catching him doodling an image of her instead of studying.

Sketches of students pepper the rest of the notebook. They're done in both pencil and ink, shaded by stippling and crosshatching, with more and more detail. First he's drawing classmates hunched over their desks, but then he begins to draw people playing soccer, basketball, and guitar. The figures are realistic and lively, his skill improving rapidly, but I'm alarmed to see that his schoolwork falls off sharply as the pages are overtaken with artwork. Video game avatars and designs of mystical creatures begin to appear in his next year's books, surely influenced by his growing interests outside of school.

When I come to the notebooks for Bao-bao's final year, I'm dismayed to find that they're half empty. Lacking both schoolwork and illustrations. It's as if he lost interest not only in his education but also his art. I remember what Min said about Bao-bao being practically addicted to video games.

The last exercise book has a plain brown board cover that's different from the others, but *Twelfth-Year Moral Education* is boldly printed on the front. I flip it open and immediately see that rather than the Communist thought essays, quotes, and theories that should be filling the pages, this book is a home for sketches. I go through the pages slowly. Elaborate drawings, portraits, and design studies cover every page. Min's nine-tailed fox is here, taking up several pages as he developed it to the final version that I found under the bed. The design starts in pencil as partial studies, the face of the fox, the sweep of the tails, the images colored different ways as if he was testing out different color schemes.

I recognize other images that started as doodles in his earlier notebooks and see how they advance to perfect works with sharp, bright colors. Bao-bao couldn't have done them all in class because there's no way he could work with an array of colored pencils and markers under the watchful eyes of a teacher.

My legs, bent under me, are tingling so I have to move. I'm holding the sketchbook as I stretch out onto my stomach, and two large envelopes slip out from the back. I stare at them for a moment, my heart beating faster, dreading at what I might find there.

I open the first one and pull out several pieces of torn, crumpled papers. They've been smoothed out, but the creases and rumples still show. I start laying out the pieces, fitting them together like a jigsaw. It takes me several minutes to figure out that they're five animals of the zodiac. The dragon, which was Bao-bao's sign, the snake, the horse, and the goat each pose fiercely against a pattern of blue and white clouds.

The last one of the monkey is only half completed. Bao-bao must have spent hours on these illustrations; they're intricate in detail and colored with complex shading. What could have made him tear them up?

I examine the monkey, looking for some flaw, imagining Bao-bao blowing up at some mistake he made and ripping them apart. Was he actually such a perfectionist? Or was he a loser who neglected his studies, shrugged off our parents, and played video games?

I open up the other envelope and draw out a thin sheaf of papers. My breath catches as I carefully flip the sheets. Dragon, horse, monkey, all the other animals of the zodiac are here, done in the same style as the torn-up ones. Bao-bao started all over and finished all twelve animals. There are a few other mythical creatures as well: dragons, phoenixes, cranes, drawn in another style. I spread them out around me.

The time he must have spent on them. How did he manage to hide all this from Mama and Baba, who clearly would've viewed drawing as a waste of time?

Was it Mama or Baba who found these images and ripped them up? I picture the fury that must have been triggered when they saw that Bao-bao's good mind was distracted from studying, that he was spending precious time doing art.

But the waste of such a talented artist is another heartbreak. I can see he worked hard at crafting his skill in secret, that he wasn't allowed to go in the direction of his heart. This is something I know more about than I care to admit.

I slowly gather the drawings and slide them back into the envelope. Although I've found no note, I feel as if I understand Bao-bao a bit more now. Which only makes the gaps in my knowledge more glaring. There's so much I will never know.

12

The next day, Baba has had a bad morning, and I'm about to clean the floor where he vomited in his room when I hear Gilbert's grandma calling to Nainai at the door. I quietly set down the bucket of clean water and pull the connecting door of the two rooms closed most of the way, because Baba has sprawled out in a restless slumber on the kang in here. Still, their voices drift in as Nainai urges her friend to enter.

Gilbert's grandma chides Nainai for not telling her about Bao-bao, but her tone is gentle. There's a brief scraping sound as Nainai goes back to peeling potatoes. She makes excuses: she just found out, they didn't tell her right away, she was shocked and too despondent to go out, knowing the family has lost face.

I swirl my rag in the bucket, hating that Nainai feels that way. Whenever something like this happens, people associate the family with bad luck. The gossip can be ruthless.

At least Gilbert's grandma is being kind. She clucks her tongue as Nainai talks. I hear her heave down onto a stool, and a clatter of ceramic as tea is made.

"Ennh! How does one go on?" Gilbert's grandma says.

"There's nothing else to do. We just have to." Nainai's voice is somber.

"Gilbert says Chen Kou is suffering in the worst way. Is he here?"

Nainai answers, but I suppose she tells her that Baba's sleeping because their voices drop. I go back to washing the floor quietly, holding my breath against the sour smell. I work slowly because I'd rather not go out there.

The floor is nearly clean when I hear Gilbert's grandma say my name and chuckle lightly. I leave the rag, crawl closer to the door, and peer out. She sits at the table sipping tea, her back to me. Her hair is roughly cut like most of the older women's, mostly gray and held back with a headband. Her neck is deeply tanned from working in the fields.

Nainai stands at the table with a potato and a metal grater in her hands. "That would be a good situation. The ideal, really, but who can think about that now?" She bears down and scrubs the potato fiercely on the grater.

Gilbert's grandma reaches over and pats Nainai's hand. "You don't need to worry about any of it. I've been telling Huan all these years, and now that he's secured this new job, it's the right time. I'm sure the seed is planted. I'll be surprised if he doesn't do something soon."

Nainai's head bobs distractedly. "Yes, yes."

"Everything has changed for your family. You've been hit with an awful affliction. But our families have always been close, and we'll try not to be as wary and . . . superstitious as some people are about these things." She leans forward onto her elbows again. I can see one of her fists urgently but softly pound the table. "Now is the time to *lock it in!* It would be something for your son to look forward to."

I gasp and quickly slap my hand over my mouth. She's talking about marriage. About Gilbert and me getting married.

I think about Min's ma and her frantic efforts to get Min matched up. I wrinkle my nose. Gilbert and I haven't even really dated. Part of me wants to laugh out loud, imagining his face when she starts in on him.

But part of me is grateful just to be thinking about something, anything, besides Bao-bao's death.

13

After Gilbert's grandma leaves I come out of Baba's room. Nai-nai is sitting at the small table, staring into her cup. She's never just sitting, not doing anything.

"Ah, Na." She glances at the bucket I'm holding. "All done? Is your baba still sleeping?"

I nod.

She pulls a smile that doesn't quite reach her eyes. "You're all grown up now. Such a help. You were always such help, even when you were as young as seven or eight. I remember when I got back from the fields you would have all the washing done and my dinner ready. And when Bao-bao—" She stops for a moment and looks away, taking a moment to collect herself before she continues. "He would be sitting here at the table doing his homework while you checked it over his shoulder and served up our food while you were at it."

I stand there with my bucket in hand, miserable, but glad that she's talking to me about him. "Nainai, why did he do it? Was he so unhappy that a bad score seemed like such a hopeless thing?"

She shakes her head, wisps of her gray hair falling over her eyes. "I don't know." She sighs heavily. "We didn't know him much after he left us, eh?"

I know what she means. Before when it was just the three of us, we were our own family unit. Nainai was our parent then. Even now, I'm more comfortable with her than I am with Mama and Baba.

"Go ahead." She swings a finger from the bucket to the door, gesturing for me to dump it in the yard. "After you dump that, you should go out for a while. I'll stay with your ba. I'm not going to work in the fields today."

I start to protest but Nainai says, "Go, go. Go see Gilbert. You shouldn't be with us old sad people all the time. Take a break. You're both going to start work soon. You should see him while you're here."

Outside, the sun is blazing. I dump the dirty water out in the lane. Nearby, three young children are scratching at the dirt with sticks. One of them, a girl in a ruffled tank top and pink plastic sandals, is using her stick to stir dirt in a can. With it being summer, there's no school, so I know these children are left to entertain themselves while their grandparents work in the fields. Of course their parents have gone to the cities. They probably only know their parents as voices over the phone.

Bao-bao and I always looked forward to our parents' yearly visits. We'd be shy with them at first, but by the time they had to go back to work, we would be terribly unhappy about their leaving.

I wouldn't show it. I couldn't, because Bao-bao would already be mad. He wouldn't want to say goodbye, and after they left and called home he wouldn't want to talk to them on the phone. I'd tell him that they were working hard for us. I'd scold him for being mad or sad. All the same things that Nainai or Mama had said to me until I started keeping everything inside. We never said we missed them, but we both did.

I put the bucket back in the yard before I head for Gilbert's. As I walk on the hilly road toward his house, the sun scorches. The countryside is still, except for the buzzing of the insects in the field. I'm not used to the quiet anymore. The loneliness and yearning I remember from my childhood creep over me. I always wanted so desperately to go somewhere, to do something. Soon enough I'll be going to Taiyuan, which I longed for back then, but now that I'll be going there to work, my heart is cold as stone.

Gilbert's two-story home is just a few years old, built from the wages his parents sent home from their jobs in the south. It sits on a hill, a boxy vertical rectangle, above their old yaodong, which Gilbert says his grandma still prefers. I'm nearly there when Gilbert comes out. I smile to see that his hair is back to normal with his bangs hanging down to his glasses.

"My nainai told me she just came from visiting yours," he says. "I hope your nainai wasn't too upset that I told her about Bao-bao."

"Don't worry," I reassure him. "It probably made it easier for her than having to tell your nainai herself."

"Is your ba doing better today? He must be since you're out."

"Nainai's watching over him. She pushed me to go out for a little bit."

"Good! Do you want to go to the village?"

I grimace, not wanting to deal with the locals asking questions or gossiping about our family behind my back.

"Of course not. How stupid of me. Let's walk over to the old school?"

I nod. We head up the lane, falling into step beside each other. The school is on a flat rise a few hills beyond the village.

We don't talk. I'm afraid that Gilbert doesn't know what to say to me, so I say, "Our nainais were talking about your new job. When do you start working?"

"Next week," Gilbert answers, but he suddenly looks down at his feet and falls silent again.

"What's the matter? Are you sorry it's not in a big city?" I know he applied for several positions, most of them in cities, but this one in Loufan is the only one he's been offered.

He sighs. "I guess I should be glad to have something. It'll be a good start, and then maybe in a couple years I can find something else and transfer to a city."

We amble on. We reach the top of a rise that looks down on terraced fields of kaoliang. Gilbert fidgets, marking the dirt with the toes of his shoes and kicking at stones. I sense that he's preoccupied. "Are you worried about something? Your job?"

He doesn't say anything at first. I notice he's sweating. He swallows, making a small noise in his throat. This is nothing like the easygoing Gilbert I know.

"What is it?" I ask.

"Na, I think . . ." The catch is back in his throat and he clears it again. He looks so uncomfortable and timid in a way I've never known him to be. "I think we should get married." He peers at me uncertainly.

I stare at him, not certain I heard right.

"I mean, will you marry me?"

My mouth flies open. His grandma really has wasted no time.

"You see, Na, now that I have a good job, I'm well positioned to get married and start a family." He looks almost as if he's going to be sick.

"Loufan is only an hour away, so we can live here with my grandparents, and I can commute to work. You'll be close to your nainai and your baba—if he stays here." His speech tumbles out in a nervous rush, his gaze jumping around to the ground, off to the distance, glancing off me.

"But I want to finish school." The words pop out before I remember that I'm not going back to college. "I mean, I'm supposed to go to work."

"I know. We can just get engaged for now. You can work a few months while I get settled in my position." He rushes on, "Maybe we can register the marriage during the Spring Festival. Won't you be twenty by then? I'm sure your parents will agree, because you'll be able to help your ba and your nainai too."

Gilbert's grandma talking to Nainai, what Baba said on the bus—I have the prickly sensation that plans about my future have been swirling around for quite some time without my even knowing about it. An odd, nervous fluttering is growing inside me. I don't know if it's excitement or uneasiness.

"Na"—Gilbert's tone shifts almost back to normal— "I know this is unexpected and maybe it's the wrong time to ask, but I wanted to speak before any more plans get made. We're both at new starting points in our lives. And we've always gotten along so well. My ma and my nainai have always liked you. They've been encouraging me to propose."

Encouraging. Pressuring is more like it. If older girls like Min get pressure from their parents, guys from the country-side suffer too. No one wants to move to the countryside, and with there being so many more men than women, finding any woman who is willing to marry someone out here, even if he has an education, is almost impossible.

"And I like you," he adds. "I've always liked you."

My heart pounds, my mind reeling to what the girls always said about Gilbert being my boyfriend. All these years, I wasn't sure how he felt. I hoped, but I never wanted to admit to them that I didn't really know.

Gilbert steps in and leans down to kiss me, but I startle, and his lips land on my jaw.

We both laugh. I cover my mouth to hold in my giddy disbelief.

"Just think about it," Gilbert says.

14

When I get home, Nainai flashes her brows at me inquisitively, but I turn away without saying anything. I don't know what to think. In less than a week, I finished my first year of college, my brother killed himself, my parents have fallen apart, I've accepted a low-paying job, and now I have a proposal of marriage. I'm bewildered. My mind can't grasp it all. All the things Gilbert said were completely sensible, but the idea of getting married when we haven't even really been a couple—I can hardly digest it.

Still, it's nice to be wanted. And Gilbert is a good guy. I want to hold this close for a while, even though Nainai obviously knows.

The very next day, Gilbert's grandma is sweeping past the doorway quilt and calling out for Nainai. My stomach drops. Nainai's gone to the market, but Baba is sitting in Nainai's padded chair in the back shadows of the room, smoking and nursing a cup of tea.

She sees me first, moves inside, and clasps my hands, squeezing them with eager little pulses. A broad smile lights her face.

"Hello!" Baba calls out to Gilbert's grandma in an overly loud voice. He puts the tea down on the floor and starts to stand.

Gilbert's grandma releases my hands and rushes over to Baba. "Don't get up!" Her face clouds with concern as she urges him to sit. "You've had a horrible shock! Aiyo!"

Baba drops back into his seat while Gilbert's grandma takes a stool from the table and moves to sit in front of him. Her face twists in sympathy, and she sways her head, making compassionate clucks. "I don't know about young people these days. The bitterness you've eaten for your boy. And he does this!"

Baba woke this morning with a numb look, the best I can hope for these days, but now his expression begins to grow long.

"But you still have Na, ennh?" Gilbert's grandma charges on. "Otherwise you'd be a shidu parent, with no one to take care of you in your old age."

Baba's mouth trembles as he sucks on his cigarette. His gloom seems to be building, so I rush to make a clatter with some mugs and ask Gilbert's grandma, "Have you eaten?"

"Yes." Gilbert's grandma jumps up and comes toward me. "Don't bother." She gestures at the tea. "I just couldn't wait any longer to come over." She is back to beaming at me so hard, my face warms. "Gilbert says the proposal went well."

I really blush now. I glance at Baba because I haven't said anything to him. Gilbert's grandma catches the look. "But you haven't told him?"

"Told me what?"

Gilbert's grandma wheels around. "Such good news! It's time for Huan to get married, and he's asked Na!"

"What?" Baba bolts upright in his seat. "What's this?" The stub of his cigarette slips out of his fingers and falls to the floor, still glowing red at the tip.

"Yes. Just yesterday!" Gilbert's grandma steps over and stamps out the butt. "You know he finished college and has gotten a good position not far from here. They can live with me here in the village!"

A look of utter surprise is on Baba's face. "Na?"

"Yes, he's just asked me," I say helplessly. "Nothing's been decided!"

Baba and Gilbert's grandma look at each other. Baba has forgotten his misery for the moment, and Gilbert's grandma looks smug with her eyebrows raised high on her forehead. She nods indulgently at me before turning back to Baba. "It's fortunate you decided she should quit school. *It's better to marry well than study well.* A little education helps, but now the girls get ambitious about their education and careers and wait too long to get married and have children."

Baba pulls a face. "But if I remember, you all were the ones who pushed us to send her to school." There's a touch of reproach in his voice.

"Yes, yes! But you see how going to the same school has developed their friendship!" She rocks back on the heels of her plastic slippers with her hands clasped at her middle, clearly pleased with herself.

Baba turns to me and sighs, "*Having a daughter is like spilled water.*"

"Not this time!" Gilbert's grandma says. "She'll be living right here at home with us. She can come over here and help your ma when you go back to work."

"And Huan—this means he won't be a *bare branch*, eh?" Baba remarks.

Gilbert's grandma doesn't seem to notice that Baba is being snide. "Isn't this the perfect kind of marriage? *Matching doors and matching windows.* Two people from the same background, and from the same village—it couldn't be more fortunate."

I feel both self-conscious and strangely absent as they talk. Baba peers at me, as if he sees me in a new way, while Gilbert's grandma eyes me like the perfectly ripe fruit ready to be plucked from a tree. I suddenly wonder if Gilbert even actually wants to marry me. He didn't say anything about love.

When Gilbert's grandma is ready to leave, Baba gets up and follows her to the door. The sun beats down on his face as he watches her cross the courtyard. When she's out of sight, he turns to me, still regarding me with that changed look. He slowly begins to nod. "It would be a good thing. Yes, really, the best thing for us."

15

Over the next week, Gilbert comes over most days. We're awkward with each other at first. Having never really had a boyfriend before, I'm not sure how to act. We don't talk about the proposal, though it's certainly on my mind.

When I have a moment to myself, I try to imagine myself as Gilbert's wife, living with him and his grandparents in their two-story house. Gilbert will be at work five or six days a week, plus the hour-long bus ride each direction. What will I be doing? Cooking, working the fields, cleaning? Those were all the things I used to do in the summer with Nainai when I came home from school.

The thought of the old arrangement, of being out here in the countryside, makes me sober, as if I would be going backwards. In past summers, I could always look forward to going back to school. I never felt I was stuck here forever.

I try to brush the unease away. If we marry, Gilbert would come home to me every night.

Gilbert doesn't push me for an answer to his proposal. Instead we're just glad to be together. There isn't much to do here. He asks me if I want to go to karaoke or shoot billiards in the village, but because of Bao-bao, it doesn't seem right to play.

As we take walks with the heat beating down on our heads in the isolated hills or pick vegetables for our grandmas from the terraced fields, we talk about school, about Bao-bao, about our new jobs, and my self-consciousness evaporates. Still, beneath my composed surface, I'm filled with wonder that Gilbert is actually my boyfriend and that we might really get married.

Bao-bao's death is still fresh in everyone's mind, and even Baba and Nainai don't bring up the potential marriage. I'm pleased that Baba always comes out to greet Gilbert and chats a little with him for a few minutes, even if he's a little unsteady. Although Baba continues to have very bad nights, his days are less tortuous. He's taken to sitting outside in the morning before the air becomes hazy with pollution blowing over from the coal mines. It seems clear that the prospect of my marriage has helped Baba, and he's making an effort to pull himself out of his despair.

❦❦❦

By the end of the week, I agree to accompany Gilbert to the village so he can get a haircut and do some shopping before he starts work on Monday. The hair salon is a tiny cluttered shop with one swivel chair in front of a mirror and another one in front of a sink. Posters of hairstyles and boards with tassels of hair in different shades cover the wall not blocked by the shelves of bottles and styling tools.

Because I always have my hair cut by Nainai or one of my roommates, I don't remember when the shop opened. The stylist seems to be about my ma's age, considerably younger than most adults living in Willow Tree. I wonder who gets their hair cut here besides Gilbert.

"Well, now it starts," Gilbert groans over the buzz of clippers when he's settled in the chair with a haircutting cape draped over him. "Work on Monday."

"You're not looking forward to it?" I say, standing behind him and the stylist, watching through the mirror as she works.

He frowns. "It has to be done, right? The money will be nice. I'm excited about that. But it's so odd not going back to school."

I take a sip of the warm Coke I'm holding and nod, knowing just what he means.

"We had so much freedom there, didn't we, once we made it to the college level? If you'd gone to an academic college you'd have been buried in writing papers and studying."

The stylist swivels him around to make the final clips around his ears. He gazes out through the window of the salon to the street. There's no one out in the heat, and the village seems lifeless and torpid.

He heaves a sigh. "Those days of playing badminton, arcades, hanging out with friends—all that's over."

I'm a little surprised to hear about this. Gilbert and I texted often, shared our bus rides to and from school twice a year, and occasionally saw each other at the canteen—but we hardly spent any time together when we were at school, even once I reached the college level and had a little more leeway since there were fewer restrictions, less supervision. I always assumed that his course load was heavier in his final year and that he didn't have much free time.

"Done!" The stylist spins him back to the mirror and whips the cape off from around his shoulder.

Gilbert twists and dips his head, studying the cut in the mirror. It's buzzed shorter on the sides and longer at the top, acceptably conventional, except his bangs are clipped to be slightly jagged, edgy. "Good!" he declares.

After he pays we head down the street. Gilbert's satisfaction with the fresh haircut is short-lived. He says wistfully, "Now our youth is all over."

"You're making me melancholy," I say just as we reach the double-stall shop that sells groceries and household items. Gilbert's phone rings right before we duck under the rollup doors.

He looks at it to see who's calling and a smile spreads over his face. "I have to take this." He rushes across the street to stand in the narrow shade of a building, well out of hearing range.

I enter the shop to get out of the sun. Products are stacked to the ceiling all around the walls and tower on the two long tables in the center. A narrow aisle loops around the tables, but a man in a sweat-yellowed undershirt—the owner, I assume—is sleeping on a mat on the floor, blocking the aisle at the back of the shop where it U-turns around the tables. An electric fan is positioned to blow on him and also to catch his wife, who sits on a stool nearby, fanning her leathery face with a folded newspaper.

I stay near the front, waiting for Gilbert, watching him as he laughs and smiles into the phone, kicking pebbles on the ground.

I'm nicked by jealousy to see him so suddenly enlivened, chatting away to some friend. For a moment, I wonder if it's a girl. But I quickly erase the thought. I have no cause to imagine that; the friends I've seen him with on campus are all guys. And the only rumor of Gilbert having a girlfriend had to do with me. Still, it stings that he's asked me to marry him, yet he seems to have a longing for his former life.

He finishes his call and walks back. His step is light and a smile plays on his face. He catches my eye and his expression flickers, as if he completely forgot I was there. He slips the phone into his pocket and crosses into the store.

"Who was it?" I ask.

"My friend from school, Guo-Rong. You met him last summer, remember? He rode home with us and visited for a couple of days before going on to his village. He's got a position in a town a couple of hours away." Gilbert grabs a plastic shopping basket and begins to scan the table piled with spicy gluten snacks, QQ gummies, and dried cuttlefish.

"That's great!" My jealousy is swept away. "So you'll have a friend not too far away."

"Yes. It will help."

"Friends make all the difference. Even on the hardest days in Linfen, when the air burned my throat and the lectures were as dry as the dust, I was happy because of my roommates," I say.

"Are you disappointed that you can't finish college?" Gilbert plucks some Want-Want crackers from a mound on the table and drops them into his basket.

I don't like that I can't finish what I've started, and that I won't get to see my friends anymore and didn't even get to say goodbye. It's like realizing I've left a half-read novel on a bus as it drives away, but I don't want Gilbert to get any more maudlin than he already is. I pull up a smile. "Eventually the girls will graduate and scatter. Everyone will go their own way in the end."

Gilbert has moved on to the grooming items. His hand hovers on a pack of razors, but he's noticed something else and is looking past me outside. I twist around to see what he's looking at.

Baba's on the far side of the street, sauntering in the shade of buildings. His arms are wrapped around Bao-bao's urn and a bottle of baijiu, and he's blinking in the way that tells me he's already drunk, struggling to stay on course.

Before I can do anything, the owner's wife comes up the other aisle and plants herself in front of the shop. "Look, there's Chen Kou," she says back to her husband over her shoulder.

The shopkeeper, rising from his nap, cranes his neck to see from the back of the stall. "He's carrying his son's ashes." He smacks his mouth and slips his hand under his singlet to scratch his belly. "It's the worst when *white hair has to send black hair first.*"

I'm rooted to my spot, my stomach turning, as Baba shuffles down the street. Gilbert and the shop owners stare too, as if we're all watching a funeral procession.

"They say the boy killed himself because of a poor score on the gaokao," the wife adds.

"Such a waste!" The shopkeeper hoicks up a wad of phlegm and spits it on the aisle floor. "That generation doesn't know how to deal with disappointment. They can't take any hardship!"

"A thing like that—the family is cursed now."

Blotches of heat spring up on my neck, my face.

Gilbert opens his mouth as if to say something to them, but I catch his eye and shake my head.

My whole face is burning, but I elbow my way past the shopkeeper's wife and hustle to catch up with Baba.

16

Gilbert starts his new job and doesn't get home until after seven-thirty. Over the next week, we only see each other briefly in the evenings because he's exhausted and his nainai nags him to rest. The days feel long without his company. I help Nainai in the fields, do the cooking and housework, try to keep Baba company. Except for the part about watching Baba, it all seems like when I was little, waiting, waiting for something to happen.

Aside from a few texts I send Mama telling her that Baba is fine, I don't hear from her until she texts me to come back to Taiyuan to start work. I haven't told her about Gilbert's proposal. The thought of talking to her about it makes me uncomfortable. Beyond her always declaring, *No boyfriends*, we've never really spoken about anything so personal.

Before I head back to the city, I duck my head into Baba's room to say goodbye. He raises his head from the pillow and blinks at me sleepily when I remind him that I'm going. "Good, good. Help your ma." I nod and tell him to try to eat more and take some walks, but he only waves at me dismissively.

Nainai follows me out to the gate, where Gilbert's waiting for me. She pats my cheek. "Won't be long before you're back here," she says, pointedly looking back and forth between Gilbert with me with a smile playing on her face.

Gilbert notices, and we both pink up. He walks me to the station and waits with me until the bus arrives. We don't hold hands or kiss because there are a few locals milling around. Nothing more has been said about us getting married, but it feels like it's set.

I arrive in Taiyuan on Sunday afternoon. Mama is at the bus station to pick me up. Her eyes are bloodshot and she looks drained as we walk back to the apartment in the heat. She tells me she's switched to the night shift so that I can take her spot on days. I start to protest, but she shushes me, saying she wants it this way and she's already started working the nights.

At first I assume that she's just trying to make working easier for me, but the dark bluish circles around her eyes tell me that she's not sleeping. I've seen how she lies awake at night, flopping around in bed with restless thoughts of Bao-bao and money worries spinning in her mind. Perhaps it will be better for her to work those nighttime hours and be at odds with the rest of the world.

As we descend the stairs to the second sublevel, I'm dizzied by the darkness. I place one hand on the wall to steady myself and force myself to take shallow breaths against the stuffy air and the feeble, blue-tinged glow from distant fluorescent lights. Will I ever get used to living down here? I keep my eyes on the back of Mama's head as I follow her to the new apartment.

When we get there, she snaps on the hanging bulb, tells me she needs to sleep, and crawls into the bed. It takes up most of the space in our new room. Mama paid a couple of coworkers to move the bigger bed and Bao-bao's desk here, and to get rid of everything else that wouldn't fit. The kitchen cart, two stools, and several boxes crowd what's left of the floor space, and it occurs to me that there won't be room for three of us here when Baba comes back to work. Will we take turns sleeping in the bed, working alternating shifts? Or does Mama not believe Baba will ever come back to work?

I lower myself onto a stool, facing the mound of Mama in the bed, not knowing what I should do with myself while she tries to sleep. Figuring the light must be bothering her, I turn it off, so now I'm in total darkness except for the red numbers of the digital clock showing 2:07 pm. It's afternoon, but it may as well be the middle of the night. The room is airless, but Mama pulls a sheet over her head. I feel as dreadful as when I first came here. Was it just two weeks ago?

I pull my phone out of my pocket and text Gilbert. *We arrived.*

I'm surprised when he texts back immediately as if he had the phone already in his hand. *Good. How was the trip? How's your ma?*

I smile at his thoughtfulness. I'm so glad to have someone to talk to.

She's so tired. I think she's been doing double shifts. Working to forget about everything.

A couple minutes pass with no response. I wonder if he's gone off to do something else.

Sometimes that's a good thing, he finally texts.

Me: *Maybe.*

Gilbert: *Don't forget. It's only been a few weeks.*

True, I answer.

Another long pause.

I don't want the conversation to be over. *I'll have to remember that*, I message, trying to draw out the exchange.

And I miss the feel of your smooth chest against mine. I can't wait until I see you again.

My head snaps back and I blink, confused by the words and the unfamiliar, passionate tone. *Smooth chest against mine?* A warm flush creeps up my neck. In all the days we were in Willow Tree, we didn't do anything more than kiss a few times. And those kisses were pretty chaste. Our chests hardly touched. I clutch the phone, acutely aware of my own inexperience, wondering what sort of response I should give.

Excuse me! Gilbert texts again before anything comes to me.

A relieved, nervous laugh escapes me, and I swiftly glance at Mama to make sure I haven't disturbed her. I'm not sure what Gilbert meant by that text, but I type, *Don't worry about it.* I'm too embarrassed to say anything more.

We'll talk more later, he answers, and I know he's signing off. I suppose he's as embarrassed as I am.

I'm left in the dark listening to the low whir of the fan. Muted noises—doors slamming, the murmur of TVs and people talking—come from the hall, the other apartments. I wish Gilbert was here. Or I was there. What did he mean by what he said? Is he longing for more from me?

I consider texting my roommate Xiaowen, to tell her that I'm not going back to school, about Bao-bao, about Gilbert's proposal, but I don't want to field her shocked questions or even her excitement about Gilbert. It's still too new. Everything has happened so fast. Of course, I always expected to get married eventually, but I'm still taking it in. I think again how even now I haven't told Mama. The fact that she hasn't mentioned it makes it clear that she and Baba aren't communicating much.

I sit for another few minutes toying with my phone before I decide I can't stay here anymore watching Mama sleep. I have to go out.

Although I try to be very quiet, as soon as I open the door, Mama rolls over and pushes up onto her elbow, alarmed. "Where are you going?"

"I'm just going out to the courtyard so you can sleep," I whisper, trying to calm her.

"Don't stay out too long. The air is bad today."

"I'll check the AQI. If it's bad, I'll come right back. Otherwise I'll get something for our dinner."

She jerks a nod before she flops back onto her stomach and burrows into the pillow.

I start toward the stairs, but suddenly I have the idea to see if Min is home.

To my sharp disappointment, she doesn't answer my knock. I head upstairs. The courtyard is teeming with families coming and going, kids playing since it's Sunday. I wonder if Min's gone to the Marriage Market to shoot more photos for her project. I decide to look for her there.

At the park, the crowd is thinning. Parents are taking down their children's profile sheets and closing up their umbrellas. I stand near the entrance of the park and wait to see if Min comes out. I don't have to wait long. I wave to catch her attention when I see her.

"Get many good shots?" I call out as I dodge park strollers to reach her.

"Some."

"How about a husband?" I joke. A group of parents standing nearby whip their heads in our direction.

Min bursts out with a laugh. "Come on. Let's go before

my ma catches up with me. She stopped to talk to another desperate mother." We head down the sidewalk in the direction of home.

"How was your village? Did you start work?" Min asks.

"Start tomorrow," I answer. My tongue begins to itch to tell her about Gilbert. She would be neutral, not family, not a friend who always *just knew it*. I'm self-conscious saying it, but I mumble, "Well, it seems I've had my own marriage proposal."

"Really?" She turns to me with a raised eyebrow. "Who is it? Someone your parents set you up with?"

"My boyfriend from college."

"I thought you said you didn't have a boyfriend."

I shrug. "I wasn't sure how he felt. The proposal's a complete surprise. He's just starting working. And I guess since I'm not going back to school, he thought . . ."

Min lets out a breathy whistle. "His parents, and yours, must be ecstatic. Have you accepted him?"

"I haven't exactly said yes, but it looks like . . . it's going to go through."

"*Looks like it's going to go through?* You don't sound very excited. Does he suit?"

"I am excited." I laugh, letting the giddiness inside me bubble into my voice. "It's just a lot to take in. And yes, he's a good match." This I can say with conviction. *Matching doors, matching windows* flashes into my mind, but really, it's more than just our shared background. Gilbert and I have always been fond of each other.

"Well, I'm glad for you!" Min smiles broadly.

"Are you?" I'm relieved. Strangely, although Min and I hardly know each other, I care what she thinks.

"Of course! If it's what you want."

"Like I said, it was just so much a surprise. Do you think I'm doing the right thing?"

She frowns and gives me a puzzled look. "I don't know. That's for you to say. People get married for different reasons. Even someone as stubborn as me can understand that." She sighs. "You're lucky to have found someone you want to marry before your parents started turning on the pressure. It really does get harder to find the right person as you get older. Even though there are so many more men than women, most of those men are uneducated or live in the rural areas."

I glance down to my feet when she says that, remembering Baba's remark about Gilbert, without me, being a *bare branch*.

"The guys worth marrying won't consider you if you have more education or make more money than they do. Especially if you've spent time focusing on your career, getting higher degrees and moving up in your job. Once you're thirty, everyone says you're too close to being past childbearing age. The three highs—high education, high income, high age. Everyone says them like they're dirty words." She shakes her head with aggravation. "Your parents must be so happy not to have to see you through the love-hunting business," she adds. "If my own mama was so lucky!"

I don't mention that I haven't told Mama, because I can't explain why. "What would your perfect husband be like?"

"Aiyo!" She mimics an old lady scolding. "I'm not worrying about that yet. I've had a few boyfriends, but I'm not getting serious. I've been saving all these years to move to Beijing and get a studio space. This project I'm working on is going to help me launch my business."

She tells me about the portraits she's been taking of women who are choosing education or career over marriage or who are waiting for a real love match. They'll be attached to their profiles, which will be statements of independence rather than the usual information about height and job and finances.

"The whole thing will be a rejection of the *leftover woman* propaganda that the government and the media have been putting out. All that pressure for us to not have such high standards, to hurry up and get married and have children as soon as possible before no man wants you, before your eggs go bad. What they're really worried about is that the gender imbalance will cause a *threat to social stability*, because the men resort to *hooliganism*—gambling, prostitution, crime—if they don't get married and relieve their urges in a socially acceptable manner. My project is meant to challenge those ideas."

"Mmmm," I say vaguely, feeling somewhat deflated, as if by getting married I'm falling for government propaganda. I clumsily try to turn the conversation back to the photos. "Will the portraits and profiles hang in your studio?" I ask, realizing I won't be able to see them in Beijing.

"Well, maybe, eventually. But I'm going to put them together for an installation in the Marriage Market first. I'm also working on a video, and I need the installation as the final scene of it."

"Will the officials let you put up something like that? It sounds controversial."

"I'm thinking about that. I still have to figure out how to get it through. The project will have to be subtle, focus on the women's hopes and dreams. I'll get the permit somehow."

She stops to remove her jacket; the nine-tailed fox peeks out from under the strap of her tank and I remember Bao-bao's drawings.

"Min, I found some other drawings that Bao-bao did!" As

I tell her about the doodles in the notebooks, the studies in the Moral Education sketchbook, and the zodiac series, Min slows her walking until she's stopped, listening intently.

"I want to take you somewhere," she says when I'm finished describing Bao-bao's work. She changes direction and pulls me down a side road.

We navigate several side streets until we're outside a storefront. "Here we are," Min says. The bottom half of the plate glass window is covered in a plastering of flyers and ad posters, but above them, *Taiyuan Tattoos* is painted on the glass. A tattoo shop. Min is the only person I've ever known who has an actual tattoo. I've never seen anyone in Linfen or Willow Tree with one. Even in a third-tier city like Taiyuan you don't generally see people on the streets with them.

Min opens the door for me. The shop is small and although the windows are grimy on the outside from the smog, plenty of diffuse light streams in. Framed tattoo designs cover all four walls. Several albums with more illustrations lie open on a long counter on one side of the shop.

At the back there's a table—cluttered with instruments and colored bottles of ink—plus a sink and a padded swivel chair like you see in a hair shop. A guy spins around on a rolling stool to face us. His hair is razored in a close, neat cut and he wears thick horn-rimmed glasses. Brightly colored tattoos cover one arm beneath his white T-shirt and snake up the side of his neck.

"Min!" he exclaims. "Where have you been? I haven't seen you in a while!"

"Been busy."

"Taking pre-wedding pictures? Have you opened your own photo studio yet?"

Min pulls a face. "The studio I open won't be for wedding photography! But I can't bite the hand that feeds me. Most of my savings comes from those shoots or the photoshopping I do for them. And I admit they're fun."

I've seen plenty of those shops where couples can rent outfits and have pre-wedding photos taken. The ensembles can range from Western-style white dresses to the traditional red qipao to fantasy ensembles like imperial period costumes or car-racing outfits, complete with fake backgrounds.

"Nothing wrong with fun, especially if it pays the rent." The guy is speaking to Min, but his gaze has wandered over to me.

"Wei, this is Na." She gestures at me. "Does she remind you of anyone?"

He studies me for a moment before he snaps his fingers. "Bao-bao. You're his sister."

"Yes."

"You look just like him."

My eyes are drawn to his tattooed arm, the intricately inked flowers, birds, and animals twisting around each other. I point to a fierce and watchful monkey inked near his wrist in the same style as the zodiac designs. "That one looks like Bao-bao's work."

He puts out his arm and rotates it. Dark ink lines the features of the monkey's face and separates each leaf behind him. The browns and greens are graded and rich. "Yeah. Where is he? He was doing some drawings for me."

I look at Min.

"Wei, Bao-bao died," she tells him.

Wei's arm drops down against his side. His expression crumbles as disbelief takes over his face.

"They say he killed himself," Min adds.

"What the fuck?" Wei jumps up. "When? He was just in here . . . I don't know, two or three weeks before the gaokao?" He flips his hand out, questioning, demanding answers. "What happened?"

I'm caught off guard by the strength of his emotion. My chest tightens. A lump forms in my throat.

"Wei!" Min grabs his arm and pushes him toward the swiveling chair.

He slumps into it and rakes back his hair. "But really? Is it true? Why would he?"

Min tells him about the gaokao and the rat poison.

"A bad score—that can't be!" One side of his mouth curls in doubt. "It doesn't make sense. He wouldn't care about that. He didn't want to go to university. Even when I told him he could major in art. He had other ideas."

Min glances at me. "Well, you know how his parents were on him to study all the time."

"No worse than anyone else's." Wei shakes his head. "He gave up on the test weeks before. He knew he wasn't going to score as well as they expected! He didn't let the pressure bother him that much."

Wei squints at me with an expectant tilt to his head as if he's waiting for me to explain. But what he doesn't understand is that I don't know anything. He is the one who is telling me about my brother.

Min says, "You know Bao-bao didn't like it when his baba came and dragged him out of the internet café. His baba made a horrible scene."

"He told me about that, but he didn't care about being humiliated in front of everyone. Yes, they had a huge fight, and yes, it bothered him to disappoint them, but he was still determined to do his own thing. I can't believe he would eat poison!"

"It is . . . strange, isn't it? Doesn't make sense." Min's smooth forehead creases.

I find myself waiting, listening, trying to understand what's going through her mind.

She catches me studying her and sighs. "But maybe the fights with your ba were getting to him more than he let on. He didn't like how upset it made your ma either. He wasn't completely selfish, even though that's what they told him. But he just knew he wasn't going to be an engineer."

"I think he must've been depressed," I say, slowly and hesitantly, aware of how little I understand about this. "I've read that depressed people can hurt themselves even if there's no clear reason why."

"If he was depressed, he must've hidden it very well," says Min. "Which I guess is possible. I'm not an expert. But it just seems so—so out of nowhere."

"He was so excited about those designs he was doing for me," Wei says, speaking in a kind of anguished daze. "He told me he was working on them!"

I find my voice. "The zodiac drawings? He finished them! I found them in his things."

"He got them done?" He leaps out the chair again. "That's great!"

"Well, I don't have them with me," I tell him. "They're back in our village. But I can bring them to you when I get a chance."

Wei brings his arm around again and gazes at the monkey clinging on his wrist. "I usually do all my own designs, but he showed me several things he drew. He came up with this one for me. I liked it so much I asked him to do the whole zodiac. He really understood when I explained how to design things so they age well. There's a certain way to draw so the ink doesn't blur as your skin gets old." He rubs his arm absently for a moment before he looks up. "I'm so glad he finished them. I can't wait to see them. When can you bring them to me?"

"It may be a while before I go back to the village. A few months, maybe." I can't ask Nainai or Baba to send them to me, because they'd demand to know everything about them. I certainly don't want to bring up things about Bao-bao that would probably upset them.

"He wanted to learn how to ink," Wei says, closing his eyes and rubbing his cheek. "I promised I'd teach him if he did the series for me. You should have seen him trying to hold back the tears when I gave him his tattoo."

"Bao-bao had a tattoo?!"

"Tiny one on his cheek." Wei points to a spot behind his left hip. "His sign, the dragon." He reaches over for an album on the table behind him and flips several pages before he finds what he's looking for. "His design, of course."

I lean over the book to see a tiny blue-green scaled dragon with flames coming out of his mouth. The mouth is wide open and appears to be smiling despite the flames that burst out and wrap around the body. "I can't believe he had a tattoo," I say.

My phone dings and I pull it out. It's a text from Ma: *Where are you?* I glance at the time. I've been gone more than an hour.

"I have to go," I say.

Wei gets up and walks Min and me to the door. Before I step out, I tell him that I'll bring Bao-bao's designs as soon as

I can. He nods and slips his arms around Min's waist. I let the door close behind me, leaving them inside, but I watch through the glass as she turns to face him. He gathers her in his arms and they kiss. Deeply. Intensely.

A blush creeps over me, and I shift my gaze to an ad for a clinic that does double eyelid surgery. As I wait for Min, my eyes are trained on the before and after images, but all the while I'm wondering why Gilbert has never kissed me like that.

17

My job at the recycling plant begins the next day. Mama walks to the bus stop with me, pointing out landmarks to help me remember the way, repeating the bus number several times to drum it into my head. The bus pulls up, and I'm surprised when Mama boards and goes with me to the plant. She explains that she's been given permission to train me the first day and will only do a half shift of her own tonight.

The plant is beyond the outskirts of the city, the last stop on this line. Everyone on board disembarks and walks the long dusty approach road to the sprawling facility, North China Scrap Metal Recycler. Mounds of material are piled under a high open-air shed, spilling out beyond its shelter. The noises of heavy machinery and the scrape of metal on metal are all around the plant. Men are shoveling the scrap into two-wheel carts and pushing them to another building, where Mama leads me.

We enter through another door and go to a locker room where we stash our purses and don green uniforms, gloves, and white cloth masks before entering the main sorting room. Here, huge square tables are piled with jumbles of metal scraps. Everything in the room is gray—the carts, the plastic bins under the tables, the high concrete walls and metal supports of the building, the second-story offices in the corner with windows that look down onto the floor. There must be more than thirty tables in the workroom, and the workers, six to eight per table, are the only dots of color.

Mama sets to work, telling me to watch her. She grabs a long pronged cultivator like Nainai uses in the fields and rakes several rusty hunks of metal toward the edge of the table. She hands me a heavy magnet and shows me how to touch it to each piece of metal.

"If it sticks, put it here." She points to a bin on the floor between us. "These are ferrous. Everything else goes in the other bin where they'll go to another table and get sorted into the different types of metal. That's my usual post."

I spend another minute listening to the *thunk*, *thunk* of metal being chucked into the bins and watching her hands fly before I take the pronged tool and get to work. Mama glances at me frequently while she works, making comments and pointing to the bins as I sort. "That one goes there, right? Okay, and that one goes in the other one. Yes! Don't get them mixed up."

She works swiftly and speaks sharply as if she's left her sorrow at home, and she is again the parent with the instructive voice on our phone. *Na, listen to what I say. Study hard. Help your Nainai.*

After an hour of monitoring my work she prods me to go a little faster. The work isn't hard, but it's dull, and after several hours I begin to lose focus.

"You dropped it in the wrong bin!" The woman on the other side of the table catches me in an error.

"Na, you have to concentrate!" Mama chides. "Work fast, but no mistakes!" For the next few hours Mama eyes me like a hawk. She clicks her tongue at me when she sees me drifting or slowing down. Despite the simplicity and drudgery of the work, her scrutiny makes me anxious, and I mess up several more times.

The day creeps along, and my back aches from standing. When my shift is finally over, Mama insists on riding the bus home with me even though she has to work another half-shift after dinner.

"But you'll have to come back right away. You won't have time to eat!" I tell her that I can find my own way, but she just shakes her head and strides toward the bus stop.

"I want to make sure you don't get lost! We'll pick up something near the complex once you know where you are, then I'll get on the next bus back here."

"Mama, I can find the way!" I'm about to point out that I'm nineteen years old and have been living essentially on my own at school for years.

"Don't argue!" The flinty quality of her tone sets me in my place, and she already has her back to me as she marches ahead. I sigh, feeling like her child. Which I am.

◆◆◆

Back in the apartment, I make some rice and eat it with a tin of salted greens. I can hear the audience laughter of a television program and the sizzle of food being cooked on the other side of the wall. Funny that scores and scores of people live down here in the sublevels. I've seen them in the halls, ducking into their tiny apartments and going in and out of the washrooms and showers, yet besides Min and Mrs. Hu, I haven't become friendly with anyone.

I suppose they all have busy lives. They work all day, come home exhausted with takeout food, and collapse in front of their screens. Or if they're young like Min, they come home and change and go back out again. I've heard the click of their hard shoes in the hallway late at night and I wonder what they've been doing—karaoke, movies, dates?

The apartment is lonely without Mama, but although I hate that she's chosen to work nights, part of me is relieved she's not here. I know that she would be grimly ruminating on Bao-bao and I wouldn't know what to do to make things better.

I text Gilbert. No answer.

I decide to try Xiaowen. When she answers my spirits revive a little, and I quiz her on what she's been doing. She's gone to stay with her parents, who work in another city. She's watching lots of movies and lots of episodes of the American television shows *Friends* and *The Big Bang Theory*.

I picture her in front of a screen, with her feet up, cracking melon seeds between her teeth. No worries to stew about. I text that I'm working now, that I won't be going back to school. I feel a finger of self-pity tickling at me, so I quickly add that Gilbert proposed, that we'll probably be getting married.

I knew it! How? When? She demands details, and giving them to her helps pull me out of my mood.

But why not finish school first?

That seems a completely practical idea. I almost don't know how to explain. I tap out the simplest answer: that Bao-bao has died, that Mama and Baba need me to work now. I push send as fast as I can.

From the long pause, I know the news is such a shock that Xiaowen doesn't know how to reply.

Oh no, how awful! I forgot how you had to rush home! She texts her condolences.

Before she can ask any questions, I change the subject. *So strange not to go back to school.* It hits me again like a hunk of metal slamming into a bin. I have no reason to go back to Linfen. But I didn't get a chance to say goodbye to any of the girls. They'll all get their degrees and find jobs where they can advance. I'll be going back to the village to wash Gilbert's socks and cook lunch for his grandparents.

Me: *We won't see each other anymore.*

Xioawen: *Maybe I can come to your wedding? When is it?*

Me: *Spring Festival?*

Xioawen: *The worst time to travel! Everyone has to be with family. I'll see what my parents say.*

She's telling me that she won't be able to come. Already my old life has disappeared.

18

Over the next week, Mama and I settle into a routine with our alternating twelve-hour work shifts. We don't see each other much, but she texts me often, especially during her meal breaks and in the morning and afternoon when we're on buses going in opposite directions.

I made soup for your dinner.

AQI 260—wear a mask!

Don't forget your lunch.

At the start, the texts make me smile because it's nice to have this daily contact with Mama. But as the week goes on, the frequency of the texts increases.

Be sure to greet the supervisor before you leave.

Ask Mrs. Hu if she needs anything when you do the shopping.

Make sure the fat on the pork is white not gray. Be in bed by 9:00.

I text back *I will* or *Thank you, Mama* each time at first, but soon I grow weary of the instructions and my responses fall off. If I don't answer, a flurry of texts appears until I do. I quickly learn I have to give at least a thumbs-up emoji so she won't worry.

This close daily scrutiny from Mama is new to me, but as smothering as it is, I realize that turning the spotlight on me must distract her from her own misery. It's little enough for me to tolerate, if it makes her feel better—but I'm glad of the hours when she returns to the floor where phones aren't allowed, because then I know I'm free until the next day.

Gilbert and I exchange brief texts too, but my long hours and the mindless sorting of ferrous and non-ferrous piles of scrap offer me nothing interesting to talk about. He seems tired as well, and his discontent at being in the countryside shows in his complaints about his boss, about having to work so much out in the bad air, about the lack of things to do for fun. The excited flutters in my stomach diminish when he talks about all that.

I work, go home, make something to eat, then get into bed, too tired even to pull out my dog-eared copy of *Anne of Green Gables*, which I always like to reread when I have time. The sounds of people moving around in the sublevel, living their lives, make me feel friendless and isolated.

In the moments before I drift off to sleep, Bao-bao sneaks into my mind like a ghost. Sometimes, bitter thoughts edge in with him. His suicide has brought me here, alone in this dark apartment, not quite filling his place as Mama and Baba's *little emperor*. Instead, I'm working in a gritty, mind-numbing job, not studying, further than I've ever been from anything I want.

Whatever that is.

I've always been a good girl, doing as my family expected, not dreaming too far ahead. I thought Bao-bao was the same way, but the illustrations I found show a different story. Many nights, those images swirl in my dreams.

By the end of the week, the unvarying pattern of each day and night has made me restless. After I've eaten my post-work bowl of instant noodles, instead of climbing into bed, I go to Min's.

"Hi! Come in." She sounds so friendly, gratitude floods me as I slip in. Her room is messy, with prints and papers scattered on the bed, but light from the desk lamp, her laptop, and the fairy lights makes the room bright and inviting.

"I'm so glad you're home!" I say. "It's too quiet in my apartment."

"Your mama sleeping?"

I shake my head. "She works the opposite shift."

"Really? Isn't that hard on her?" Min gathers the papers off the bed and gestures for me to sit. "She must hardly see you."

I shrug. "She prefers it, I guess. She's having such a hard time, work is the only thing that helps her to forget what happened to Bao-bao. For a little while at least."

Min swivels her desk chair to face the bed. When she sits, she folds one leg under herself. "How's it been for you?"

"She's been checking in on me a lot. All kinds of reminders, instructions . . ."

"Ah! I meant, how's the work, but I'm afraid you mean your ma has taken you in hand now." She grimaces sympathetically. "Well, I suppose with living apart all these years you're not used to having the constant . . . *guidance*."

I nod. "I guess this is what it must have been like for Bao-bao."

"Of course! Probably worse. You were lucky to be at school on your own, not having your parents watching every move you make. What did your ma say about your engagement?"

I draw in my lip for a moment. "I haven't told her yet. When I first got here she was too tired to talk. Every day since then it's been work, work, work so I haven't had a chance to bring it up."

"Really? But you know it will make her so happy. Or at least give her something to think about other than your brother.

Maybe it'll help her get a little bit past it. And you must be bursting with the news."

I give a half nod.

"No? Are you having second thoughts?"

"I don't know." I sigh. "It's just so unexpected, doesn't seem real."

"It does seem sort of like a *flash marriage*. But that's not too unusual these days," Min says.

"I still haven't really said yes. Gilbert doesn't push. He's giving me room to think, but it seems like the right thing to do. Like you said, Gilbert *suits*. And if nothing else, getting married would have to be better than sorting metal twelve hours a day, six days a week!"

Min winces. "Sorting metal! That's terrible. You've had a year in college, you should look for something else."

"Coal operations technology is sort of specific. And I'll probably be getting married in six months."

For several moments Min doesn't say anything, and I'm aware of how my words, with their feeble tone, hang in the air. She tilts her head, studying me. "What do you want to do?"

No one has ever asked me that. I only shrug again and flip up my hands.

She brings her leg out from under her and taps me lightly with it. "No, really. Tell me."

I root around for an answer and say the first thing that comes to mind. "Go to school first."

"And finish your degree in coal operations technology?"

I wrinkle my nose. "Well, once I wanted to study English," I admit. "Or literature."

Min's eyebrows shoot up. "I don't suppose they had that at your school."

I laugh. "No, they didn't. But in middle school, English was my favorite subject."

"Well, why didn't you take the social sciences track in school and go on to a university?" Min asks.

I look down, my gaze falling on her slippers. They're robin-egg blue, made of real leather and shaped like the ones ballet dancers wear. It's too much to explain to someone like Min that I was lucky to even go to vocational high school. "An English or literature degree is completely impractical for someone like me."

"That's our parents talking. Look at me. My parents wanted me to work in computers or medicine. When I got my degree in communications, they pushed me to take a position as a publicity rep with a big company. I did that for a few years—*riding a donkey to find a horse*. With that, and the photography on the side, I've saved up and in a couple of months I'm going to open my own studio in Beijing. And not a wedding photo shop."

"That's wonderful!" I'm impressed and glad for her, yet the smile on my face is stiff. Her situation is different than mine. Her parents piled all their resources on her and gave her all their attention. She grew up as a singleton in a city, with easy entry to the city schools, which are always better than the ones in the countryside. She didn't have to work in the fields, look after her little brother, or cook meals and wash clothes.

"Look at these!" She turns her computer screen toward me. "These are the images I'm using in my installation for the Marriage Market." She scrolls through several headshots of women without makeup, their hair down, their shoulders bare.

"Min, they're beautiful!" The photos are stark, each woman glowing and natural.

Min then rifles through some papers on her desk and hands them to me. "And these are their statements."

I take them and begin to read.

I don't want to get married just to be married.

I have a great career and I enjoy my single lifestyle.

I haven't finished living out my youth.

I press my lips together, my enthusiasm faltering. I wonder if Min is trying to tell me something. "Do you think it's the wrong thing for me to get married?"

Min clacks her tongue impatiently. "No! I told you the other day, it's not for me to say. If you want to get married for love, for security, or for your parents' sake, that's up to you! I'm not judging you for choosing the one lifestyle that society tells us is acceptable." Her tone sounds harsh, but after a moment her expression softens.

"I'm sure you have enough pressure on you, like we all do. I get it. I'm not immune to that either. I know what my parents gave me, what they've gone through, how they put all their hope on me. I know they can't rest until they see me married off and with a child. It's hard to disregard that, even if their expectations, everyone's expectations, are so oppressive."

She looks back to the photos on her computer, idly clicking through the portraits. "I know I told you this installation is to help my business. But a big part of why I'm doing it is for my parents. Even though it looks like I'm rejecting their ideas, I want to impress them. If the project helps my business, maybe they can stop worrying so much."

"Mmm." I'm doubtful Min's ma will ever back off until she's married.

"The YouKu video I'm working on is turning into sort of a short documentary. I want it to be subtitled in English. I was actually wondering if you would help me translate the women's statements and the script. I could do it myself but I have so much to do between working and the two projects . . ."

"Really? Me?" I'm excited by the idea, but all my English past middle school has only been self-study.

Min digs around on her desk. "Just do the best you can. Anything you can get done would be great. I can fix up anything you can't figure out." She pulls out some papers and shoves them at me.

"I'll take your photo sometime, if you like." She gestures to the computer, the portraits of the women still on the screen. At first I wonder if she's offering to put me in the installation, and I start to panic over what my statement would be, what my parents would think—but just as quickly, I see that being in the project wouldn't make any sense if I'm marrying Gilbert.

"Or your wedding photo." Min smiles at me. "Funny," she says. "Bao-bao wanted to do art and you want to do English."

I dismiss the impossible notion with a sniff. "Yes, and look at Bao-bao now." I flinch as soon as the words are out of my mouth. "Suicide." I say it under my breath, still so unreal.

Min pinches her lips, and that crinkle of doubt is back between her brows. "Well, if Bao-bao killed himself, it wasn't the pressure that got to him."

A prickle goes up my back. "What do you mean *if*?"

Min stares at her hands for several seconds. She exhales a resigned breath. "Nothing."

"No. What is it?" I want to know what she could possibly be thinking.

"Maybe I didn't really know Bao-bao, but he wasn't like the study kids and *test monsters* you read about online and in the papers, the ones who break under the pressure. He seemed to be pushing away from the conventional life."

She pauses for a moment, her gaze going over my head to the middle distance. "No, not pushing, so much—but more like stepping away. Your parents were giving him a hard time, but he was deflecting them in his own way. He knew their intentions were good and that they had *eaten bitter* trying to get the family ahead. But to Bao-bao, having a better life didn't mean getting a good job, apartment and car. I can't imagine that his score would've felt world-ending to him. If anything, I would've expected him to feel kind of relieved—free to focus on a different path."

Freedom is a strange thing . . .

"I still can't believe he killed himself," she says darkly, not with dramatic astonishment as Gilbert and I, who weren't close to Bao-bao, have said it. Her voice is grave, doubtful, with a timbre that sends a shiver up my spine.

"Min, what do you think happened to Bao-bao?" I ask.

"I don't know." She gives me a helpless look. "I . . . I just don't know."

19

I stay up late the next two nights translating the statements and Min's script for her video, which includes interviews with women and their parents. The hours slip away as I pore over them, consulting the tattered Chinese-English dictionary and English workbooks I've carried with me since middle school and wording and rewording the sentences until I have them sounding right.

I'm far from done, but I'm beginning to see the overall shape and tone of the project. Some of the women are already *leftovers*, past thirty, and despite their brave words—*I'm accustomed to being single; Tolerating loneliness is better than marrying the wrong man; Ma and Ba, I will support you even if I don't get married*—I see a vein of isolation running through them.

Or maybe the sad realization that it's near impossible to have it all—an ambitious career, a love marriage with a successful and supportive partner, kids, *and* satisfied parents—because the expectations are too overwhelming. Even Min admitted she can't help but care what her parents think.

It confuses me, the thrill of working with language, imagining the career I really want, yet seeing the sacrifices that other women have had to make to keep moving with their education and professions. Although I may not have those things,

I realize that by getting married, at least I won't have to worry about loneliness or disappointed parents.

Today is Sunday, so Mama and I are both off work and awake at the same time in the midafternoon. After we've eaten a late lunch of rice porridge and after I've washed the bowls down the hall, Mama tells me to call Baba. I perch on the side of the bed, dial him up and hold the phone out to her, but she thrusts out her hands, clutching a bowl and the drying rag, to show me that she can't take it.

Nainai answers.

"It's me, Nainai. Have you eaten?" I put her on speaker so Mama can hear.

"Yes. Already eaten."

"How's Ba?"

"He's sleeping. I picked up the phone so he wouldn't wake up. You started work, then? How is it?"

"Fine."

"Make sure you—"

There are noises in the background, and I hear Baba bellowing to Nainai. She tells him it's me on the phone.

"He's coming," Nainai says. Several long moments pass as Nainai tells him to hurry. I hear him muttering and can practically see him lumbering over to Nainai, near the door where the reception is best.

"Na!" he shouts into the phone, his voice warbly. I wonder how much he's drunk. "First work week, eh? Did you perform well?"

"Yes, Baba. It went fine."

"Good, good. I'll be back soon." He sounds almost ebullient, and I throw Mama a hopeful look. She keeps her eyes on the bowl, rubbing it slowly although it must be long dry.

"Your mama happy about your marriage?" Baba asks.

Mama's head shoots up, and she throws me a look of utter bafflement. I still haven't told her.

"We've been so busy with work, our different shifts . . ." I stutter into the phone.

"What's he talking about?" Mama rises. Before I can answer, she steps over and leans into the phone. "It's me," she says to Baba. "Marriage? What's this about?"

"Na's had a proposal from Gilbert! He graduated college and started work not far from here."

Mama turns her bewildered eyes on me, too surprised to say anything.

"I haven't answered him," I say uneasily. I really don't know why I haven't told her. I suppose I've been avoiding it because we've never really talked about personal things.

"Don't talk nonsense," Baba says. "It's a good match, eh Ma?" There's a pause, and I hear him smack his lips, Nainai muttering a reproach. He's drinking.

"Gilbert?" Mama hesitates as if trying to get it to sink in, but in the next moment she says, "But I told you no boyfriends!"

"We weren't really . . ." It strikes me as ridiculous that I'm almost twenty years old with a marriage proposal and I'm defending myself over old rules. "It came as a surprise."

Baba chimes in. "Ah! Doesn't matter, doesn't matter. You have to accept! Eh, Ma. Gilbert's a good match. He already has a job with potential to move up. His family already has a good house. The wedding can happen at the Spring Festival when both families are home. Our grandchildren will be coming along soon!"

My mouth goes dry. Wedding. House. Children.

Mama, still clutching the bowl and rag, plops down on the bed. She looks up at me again, her head swinging slowly with disbelief, dissent, I'm not sure which. "But she just started this job," she says, raising her voice so Baba can hear. "What about the money we owe Mrs. Hu? And the wedding will cost . . ."

Money owed to Mrs. Hu?

"Puh! Don't worry about that!" says Baba. "Gilbert's family will pay a bride price. And I'll be back to work soon." There's aggravation in his voice, and I fear he'll soon cross over to the next level of drunk. I want the conversation to be over.

"Baba, have you eaten?" I ask. "Please eat something."

"Yes, yes," he says impatiently. I doubt it's true.

"Baba, you have to take care of yourself."

"Yes!" He wants to get off the phone now as well. We say goodbye and click off.

Mama stares at the fan on the floor, watching it rotate side to side. Her expression is cloudy with vexation, suspicion as to why I haven't told her earlier, but I also know she's deliberating, weighing out options.

I find myself waiting to hear what she has to say. Will she think getting married is a good idea, or will she forbid it? The funny thing is that I'm not sure which one to hope for.

"I can't disagree that it's a good match," Mama finally says. "But—I thought you'd work a couple of years before you get married." Her eyes run over me, slowly taking in my hair and face, appraising me like the parents in the Marriage Market.

"Mama, what about this money we owe Mrs. Hu?" I ask tentatively, wanting to change the subject and hoping she might be distracted just enough to answer me. "How much is it?"

Her chest rises as she takes in a large breath. "Almost four months' salary."

I inhale sharply. "So much!" I can't keep the shrill dismay out of my voice. "How is it so much?"

She rubs her cheek. "She's helped us. Loaned it to us—for Bao-bao."

"But still, how did—!" I feel sick. "Mama, you just caught up with the rent!"

Her hands slide down to her throat, and she tilts her head back, closing her eyes for several moments. I'm sure she's not going to answer, but I wait until she opens them, and I lean in expectantly.

"Expenses with his education. We were struggling to keep up even after we moved to the sublevel apartment last summer. Over the years, tuition, books, uniform fees, gifts for teachers, afterschool test prep classes . . ."

She's mentioned all these expenses before, but I always assumed she and Baba could afford them. My chest tightens as my mind races, trying to calculate how long it will take to pay all this back.

"This final year we had to pay for even more extra classes, tutoring, and gifts to administrators and teachers because your brother was letting himself fall behind." She bites her knuckle for a moment, gathering herself. "We rented a hotel room to be closer to the testing site those three days. Such waste!" Her mouth pinches, and I see that there's anger in what she says. She springs off the bed and the bowl rolls off her lap, landing with a clack of plastic against concrete.

I bend to pick it up while Mama paces like a caged animal, three steps back and forth, all the space in the room. Except for the amount, she hasn't told me anything I didn't already know, and now I'm sorry I made her go back to her worries.

"And after he died we had to pay—" Her face goes ashen white, so white it scares me.

"Mama, never mind! We'll make it up soon enough." I try

to sound light, but the thought of our debt has embedded itself like a tumor inside me.

She ignores me but stops pacing. Her face is stretched back tight. I can see she is lost in fretting.

"Mama, let's go out." I move toward her. "Come take a stroll. Or we can sit in the courtyard."

A short tick of her head tells me she heard me. I gather her purse and urge her to put on her shoes.

Outside, the nebulous skyline of the city center in the distance is faintly visible. I guide Mama across the courtyard and out to the street moving swiftly, hoping to drive the bad thoughts out of her head. I chatter, checking and reporting on the AQI, asking her what we should cook for dinner, commenting on the things in the stores we pass.

On Jianshe Avenue I see Min walking toward us. Mama and I are headed in the direction of the park, and Min must be coming back from taking more photos of the Marriage Market, since her camera bag is slung across her body.

Min catches sight of me, notices Mama. I think about introducing them, but Min just gives me a faint nod and looks away. I'm glad that she passes. It's not the right time. Mama would've had endless questions, and I can't imagine how I would explain our friendship without it somehow leading to Bao-bao.

At the park, the Marriage Market is closing down as we weave through the thinning crowd. People are closing up umbrellas and removing profile sheets from the fences, and Mama slows down to watch. She stops in front of a bench and begins to examine a sheet. We're only there a few seconds before a man holding a profile sheet at chest level taps Mama on the shoulder.

"Is this your daughter?" he asks, pointing toward me with his chin.

Surprised, Mama nods.

He moves his head as if trying to put me in focus through his bifocals. "What's her zodiac sign?"

Mama merely blinks at him, confused as to what he wants.

A few others crowd around as he shifts his questions to me: "Are you married? In college? How many blind dates have you been on?" His voice is deep and sonorous, drawing more people's attention. He thrusts his son's profile up at Mama and me and begins to point out his son's salary and two-bedroom apartment.

The parents around us begin to comment and push in with their own questions and stat sheets.

I deflect the questions, trying to be polite, and slowly, Mama begins to understand. She turns her gaze on me once again, studying me as if she's seeing me for the first time.

"She's engaged!" Mama declares firmly, cutting off the questions.

The parents huff and immediately drift away, and Mama steers me out of the park.

Mama is quiet the rest of the afternoon as we clean the apartment and make dinner. Her eyes light on me again and again, and I sense a shift in her mood. She's lost in thought, but not with the brooding, anxious air of the last weeks. Instead, she scrubs the floor and chops the vegetables with a briskness that reminds me of her old self.

After we eat and get the dinner dishes cleaned, she asks me to get Gilbert's ma's number. I text Gilbert, telling him that Mama wants to speak with his ma. When he responds, his text contains only the number, no comment attached, and I wonder if he's as nervous as I am.

My stomach flutters as Ma dials up Gilbert's ma. I busy

myself with changing the bedsheets, though my ears are straining to catch every word.

After a loud burst of greeting from both ends of the line, Mama goes quiet and her head bows forward as she rubs her forehead. I hear Gilbert's ma chattering softly through the line and I'm sure she's giving her condolences about Bao-bao. Mama only makes a small noise to let her know she heard before she steers the conversation to the marriage.

Gilbert's ma's voice blares on the phone, "We had it in our minds all these years that Na would be a good match for Huan! I've watched her every year at Spring Festival. A good girl! Never too demanding. Not too pretty, smart enough to be sensible, and having had a sibling, she was never spoiled!"

Mama chuckles and tells her about the Marriage Market, describing the throngs of people and the profile sheets covering the park. "And so, so many men looking for wives! It was like the village livestock market." She doesn't mention that it was mostly the parents who were doing the looking. "I'm glad she doesn't have to go through finding a match."

Gilbert's ma *tsks*. "Yes, after what her brother did . . ." Mama jerks the phone away from her ear, staring at it in her hand, clearly surprised and offended.

"Our family discussed it," Gilbert's ma continues. "Even if most people wouldn't consider Na with your family's situation, we've lived in the city long enough to look past those old beliefs. We've always hoped for Huan and Na to make a match, and we won't let this change that."

I bristle. Mama and I look at each other. We both realize that she's talking about our family being cursed by Bao-bao's suicide. I have a bad taste in my mouth. I almost expect her to start haggling for a low bride price.

"Yes, the young people have to be more open, especially all the men who live in the countryside, eh?" Mama's voice is sticky sweet, but her jaw is rigid. She's speaking with a forked tongue. "Na could probably find someone richer and more educated than Huan. Several parents came right up to ask about her at the Marriage Market. Every man wants a wife willing to set aside her own education and take care of the house and children. Young wives are the best. But still, like you said, Na and Huan have a good connection."

Even though Mama's comments prick at me in their own way, she's bragging about me, standing up for me, and I can't help but feel a surge of satisfaction.

20

Each night over the next week, after I get home from the scrap metal plant, I crouch on a stool and use the bed as a desk, laboring over the translation of Min's project. Most of the time, I'm completely absorbed in a way that makes me think I can stay up all night, but every now and then when I get stumped on a sentence, I begin to doubt my abilities or the accuracy of my work. I have to push down those thoughts and tell myself to just keep going, figure out one more word, one more phrase.

I'm so busy that I only manage to send Gilbert a handful of texts, but he understands. He says he's tired from work and doesn't have the energy for much conversation himself.

When I finally get the script finished I go to Min's, but she doesn't answer the door that night or the next. Soon I won't be able to go over because Mama has decided to switch back to working days, so in the evenings I'll have to be home to make her dinner and keep her company. I end up slipping the pages under Min's door with a note explaining Mama's change in schedule.

Mama's mood is definitely brighter now. She smiles sometimes, and we take walks in the evening. At one point, we stop in front of a wedding photo shop and Mama gazes at the outfits:

sock-hop skirts, Western formalwear, and a princess ball gown and tux splayed out jauntily in the window. Photos of couples in other outfits are propped at the foot of the display against jeweled high heels and saddle shoes. Mama actually lets out a laugh as she scans them, pointing to a formally dressed couple standing on the moon.

I can't help but laugh as well, not just at the couple's fantasy backdrop, but because it's like a sack of coal has been pushed off my shoulders to see Mama so lighthearted.

Two weeks later Mama is working overtime and I go to Min's, eager to see what she thought of my translation work.

"Na!" Min says as she opens the door. "You've been sprung!"

"Yes, Mama's working late," I say with a twinge of guilt. Mama raised her hand for the shift when the foreman asked for overtime volunteers this afternoon. I begged her to go home and tried to pull her arm down before the foreman spotted her, but she said we needed the money. I told her I would do the shift, but she absolutely refused to let me take it over.

Of course I didn't *want* to work overtime. The day was already brutally long, and my muscles were strained, and I felt like I could practically taste rust on my tongue. I was glad to go home, but I hate that she's working so hard.

"I'm just on my way out," Min says. "I'm going to look at a space for my studio. Do you want to come with me?"

"Sure! But I thought your studio was going to be in Beijing."

"Yes, well, that was the dream, but rent there is about six times as much as Taiyuan. Even here, I thought maybe I could buy something, but the prices are just too high." She grabs her bag and keys and steps out into the hall. "Ma and Ba always said they were saving to help me buy an apartment, but that's only if I get married. I may have to settle for renting a space here." Her shoulders hike up in a shrug. "I can do well in Taiyuan. I have contacts here."

She starts to lock the door but says, "Oh wait. I have a book for you."

When she opens the door again and switches the light back on, my eyes fall on two books lying on her desk. One is *You Should Marry Before You're Thirty*, the one I saw her ma thrust on her. The other is *Don't Marry Before You're Thirty*.

I wait to see which one she reaches for, but she ignores both of them and reaches up to the shelf above the desk and grabs another book. Back in the hall, she shoves it at me and locks the door. "We have to hurry or I'll be late for the real estate agent."

We speed down the dingy hallway and up to the lobby. "We have to take a Didi Chuxing, though it isn't too far. I've already ordered it," Min says, and we run across the courtyard to the street, where a car is flashing lights.

Once we're in the car, submerged in cool drafts from the air conditioning, Min gives the driver the address, and I read the title of the book she handed to me. *Jane Eyre.*

"We read it in college." Min settles back in the seat as the car dips into traffic. The driver turns up the music, a slow song I recognize called "Breeze Rain."

"I've read it too," I say. "At least an abridged version."

"Well, keep it. This one's the full bilingual edition." She reaches across, flips the book in my hand, and shows me the English side. "I was supposed to read it in English, but that took too long because the story was so good. I couldn't help racing through it, in Chinese."

"Really!" I say. "I'm surprised you like such a romantic story. You don't seem very sentimental."

Min laughs as if she agrees. "Well, it's more than just a romance! When was the last time you read it? You should have another look. There's the part when Jane might marry her friend the missionary. Maybe you'll find it helpful for your situation."

I vaguely remember St. John, whom Jane loved only as a brother. He wanted her to marry him so they could be of service as a missionary couple. Is that Gilbert and me?

Min rattles on, "Jane always insists on doing her own thing. Having her freedom. My grandfather had a forbidden copy during the Cultural Revolution. Jane was revered as a hero to the repressed because she was an orphan with a hard upbringing. And even though she was very good, she would stand up to the unfair authority figures in her life and always hold her ground. We talked about that in class. A feminist heroine. Though of course in the end she marries Mr. Rochester."

I look down at the book, fingering the worn cover. I can't help but get the impression that Min is telling me that I shouldn't get married, that I should struggle more to pursue my dreams, but I don't really know what those are specifically. "Yes, because she was passionately in love him, and she wanted to marry him."

My mind veers to the heated kiss between Min and Wei. I fidget, once again aware of how nothing like that has happened between Gilbert and me, how we've actually spent very little time together.

Min sees that I'm bothered. "What's the matter?" she asks.

"Nothing." I'm too embarrassed to explain my confusion about Gilbert, that in some ways it seems I still don't know him all that well, that I don't know what I'm doing. I'm conventional and unambitious, and if I've ever had any spirit or courage like Jane, I've always kept it pent up inside. I smile stiffly.

"Oh Na. It's just a book. I know you like to read, and isn't the true value of a book whatever you take from it—your own interpretation?"

I nod, easing my smile into a real one before I turn to look out the window. Of course she doesn't mean to make judgments. It's me who is always expecting them.

The car turns down a side street and draws up to the curb. The neighborhood is nondescript, white tile and brick buildings of five or six stories with laundry hanging in the open windows. Not the glossy new neighborhood I imagined Min would seek out.

The agent is waiting for us on the sidewalk outside a small storefront with an awning and papered-over windows. The building is flanked by a small convenience store on one side and a stall shop on the other. My eyes are drawn to the stall's plastic shoes and slippers, in every color imaginable, lined up on the floor, on tables, and even on the walls. These are the only places that seem to be open, their light spilling out onto the sidewalk while the rest of the narrow street is dark.

We go inside. The agent flips on the long fluorescent tubes that run high along one wall. I walk around while Min chats with him about rates, fees, and utilities. The space is longer than it is wide, but still small, probably not much bigger than the convenience store. The ceiling plaster is cracked, and the once-white walls are dingy and yellowed. Aside from a dust-layered wooden counter near the door, the space is empty.

When the agent goes outside to smoke, Min says, "Everything costs so much! This place isn't even really in the district I want to be in, and it's even more than I expected!" She heaves out a frustrated sigh. "I could probably afford it, but maybe it's better to save up some more."

Unable to offer any advice, I give her a sympathetic look.

She goes to the window and flicks aside the paper to peer outside. "I'm pretty sure it's northern light, which makes it easier to control the lighting here inside. I could put a backdrop screen and studio lights here by the window. At the back I'd have room for a big worktable, and shelves to store equipment."

As she stalks around the room gesturing to different spots, I picture her adjusting the lights, pointing her camera, signaling to her subject to move this way or that. "I can imagine it just the way you describe. You should do it, Min. You said you've been planning on this for years."

"The space itself is pretty good. But I don't know." She goes around once more, looking the space over again. "He wants six months' rent at once. I'd better keep looking."

We go outside and she tells the agent she's going to hold off on taking the space. After he's locked up the building and leaves, we walk slowly back to the busy avenue that leads toward our district. Min is very quiet, deep in thought, her gaze shifting from the pavement beneath her feet to the storefronts and signs. Everything is lit up, making the night almost as bright as day. I imagine she's still mulling over her decision. She must be sharply frustrated to be so close to realizing her dream and still have fallen short, but it seems to me she has the boundless ability to conjure up whatever she desires.

I glance at her, ready to tell her how much I admire how much she's already accomplished—breaking from a conventional life, resisting her parents' influence, creating art exhibits, and deftly conversing with real estate agents about leases, but she abruptly quickens her pace and heads toward a vendor selling kebabs at the next corner.

"How many do you want?" she asks me.

I put up two fingers, and the vendor hands the skewered meat to me over the grill of her cart. I dig into my pocket for money and start to hand it to the vendor, but Min slaps my hand. "Put your money away!"

"No, no! Let me get it!" I slip my bill past her arm. "You have your studio to worry about." She makes an exasperated noise and we squabble for a few moments, both of us thrusting money at the vendor, who watches us with a bored expression. She finally snatches Min's bills.

"I just thought of something," Min says as we stand on the sidewalk nibbling at the kebabs. Pedestrians skirt around us. "A friend of mine from university studied in the US, and now she has a company for students in foreign countries to learn Chinese online. You know, like the internet English classes Bao-bao used to take, only these classes connect you with a native speaker."

"Sure." I raise my eyebrows, waiting for her to go on.

She polishes off her kebab and tosses the skewer into the street. "Her classes focus on simple conversation for travelers and students wanting conversation practice. Maybe she could use another tutor."

"Are you looking for more work so you can afford the studio?" I ask.

"Not me! You." She laughs and shakes her head. "Forget about the studio. You said you were interested in English. The translations you did were very good by the way. That really helped me out. I could introduce you to my friend. Give you a recommendation."

My eyes widen. I'm pleased by her praise, but the thought of interviewing, of teaching, is unexpected. "But I don't have a teaching degree."

"I don't think that matters," Min says. "If I remember, she said her courses are different because they provide mostly simple Chinese conversation to help people practice speaking. All the lesson plans are already made—different situations like eating out, asking for directions, basic social conversations."

"Well, that seems easy enough, but how does that relate to English? I'd be teaching Chinese."

"Students in the US aren't as disciplined as students here, and you'd probably get to use your English to explain things."

"I like the idea, but I already have a job. I can't give it up and take the risk that this wouldn't work out."

"No, I didn't mean quit your job. Because of the time difference you could teach some after your shift. Do it as side work."

"Hmm." I give a half-smile, uncertain.

"Let's duck into a café and WeChat her before we get back home," Min says as she starts walking.

I trip after her, feeling a stirring in my chest. I'm self-conscious about my spoken English. I can't envision myself teaching, speaking to people on the other side of the world, but she makes it sound so easy, so practical, that I can't help wondering if it's actually possible.

21

Before I know it, I've done the WeChat interview and have gotten hired on to teach one student a day, starting next week. On Sunday, I tell Mama.

She's squatting next to the laundry, searching for a clean shirt, but her head pivots in my direction.

"What's this? Teaching? What do you know about teaching?"

"It's just saying what's written in the lesson plan, Mama. The foreign students practice speaking Chinese, and they hear the language from a native speaker. I don't need any special training."

She tucks her chin back against her neck, eyes narrowing with suspicion. "Talking with foreigners online. It doesn't sound safe. They may be trying to trick or defraud you!"

"No, Mama. It's a legitimate company!"

"Where did you hear about this job?" She stands up, a shirt gripped in her hand.

I knew she was going to ask this, and I have a small lie prepared. "A school friend told me about it. Her friend owns the company." If I had just said *friend* instead of school friend, Mama would have demanded to know more.

"How much does it pay?"

When I tell her she frowns. "It isn't worth it. You can make more doing overtime at the plant."

It's true, the money is a pittance and teaching only five hours a week won't amount to much. "But I *want* to do it. It won't interfere with my work at the plant, since my teaching hour will be early in the morning before my shift." I leave out the fact that I'll have to go to the internet café and hope she doesn't ask. "I'm just going to try it out," I ramble on, trying to dodge more questions, "and the work will probably dry up in the fall when the young students go back to school."

A glaze comes over her face and she turns away to put her shirt on. I wish I could take back that last piece about students going back to school. I have to remember how everything reminds her of Bao-bao.

"Mama, I'm going to call Gilbert and tell him about it."

Hearing Gilbert's name brings her focus back to me, and her head bobs automatically in agreement.

I'd rather go outside for privacy, but Mama is always pleased to hear me talk to Gilbert. I ring him up and he answers.

"Hi." I smile into the phone and glance at Mama. She's watching me out of the corner of her eye, and I see her dimple up as she dumps the laundry on the bed and starts folding it.

"What are you doing?" I say to Gilbert.

"I'm in Changyu Township waiting for a friend."

"Guo-Rong?"

"Yes. Changyu Township is halfway for us. We've met up a couple of times to talk about old times," he says.

I grin, since the "old times" of college days were just over a month ago. I know how he misses his life in Linfen, same as I do.

"It's been great having someone young here to talk to," he says.

It's wretched that he's stuck out in the countryside. Next year I'll be back there as well. A knot tightens in the pit of my stomach as I see myself working in the fields, taking care of Baba and the grandparents

I remind myself how Gilbert said he's determined to work his way back to the city. And until then he'll be home every evening, rushing in to sit between his grandparents and me for dinner, and afterward we'll take walks or watch TV together. It won't be too stifling.

I tell him about the language class I'll be teaching, but my mind is racing ahead wondering if I can keep teaching once I'm back in Willow Tree.

"That's great!" Gilbert says with the enthusiasm I was hoping for. He's happy for me, and when he doesn't ask how much I'll be making, I know he understands that I'm not doing it just for the money.

"Yes, it is great, isn't it?" I echo his word, making sure Mama hears so she understands that Gilbert more than approves. "I'm just on a trial to start," I add, "but if I get good ratings, I might be given more students in the evening or on my day off. I'll have mainly kids. Right now she mostly needs someone to do the early morning slots when it's the afternoon in America."

"I remember how much you used to love your English class—maybe you'll sneak in some practice, huh? Listen, I'm really happy for you, but here's Guo-Rong. I have to go. I'll text you later."

"Okay, bye," I say brightly, although he's already clicked off. I turn to Mama to make sure she's been listening. Her back is to me again, but I know she heard every excited word I said.

∗∗∗

The morning of my first lesson, I wake at 3:45 to the low hum of my phone alarm under my pillow. I slip out of bed, grope for my clothes where I laid them last night, and dress as quietly as I can, careful not to wake Mama. She only tosses a bit as I open the door, and I'm outside before 4:00 a.m.

The city air glows a yellow-orange from lights of buildings, signs, and streetlamps cutting through the smog. The court-yard and streets are desolate and quiet, with only the occasional rumble and thump of a vehicle hitting a pothole. The internet café is just a ten-minute walk, and I'm not due to get online until 4:30, but I want to give myself plenty of time.

I've only passed two other apartment complexes when I hear someone call out, "Where are you going this time of night?"

I jump, nearly startled out of my skin, and wildly search for the voice. A thickset silhouette appears in the narrow backlit alley between two of the high rises.

"It's me—Mrs. Hu! Isn't that Na?" She takes several steps into a pool of light in the building's ungated courtyard, drag-ging a large bag of recyclables, the scrape of it echoing off the concrete.

I blow out a breath. "Yes! You scared me!" I venture into the courtyard. Her cart is in the shadows, and back at the far end of the alley, I can see Mr. Hu, picking through the bins.

"What are you doing out now? It's not even—" Mrs. Hu checks her watch—"four in the morning!"

"I'm going to work." I grin, hearing the note of pride in my own voice.

"Aren't you working at the scrap plant with your mama?"

"I am, but I have a side job teaching English. I'm going to the internet café."

"English! Really!" Her mouth curls up, briefly impressed, before it rearranges into a frown. "Are you sure you're not going there to play video games?"

I make a face.

"I suppose not." She swipes at some gnats buzzing near her face. "That's a boys' thing, eh? Good. That would be the death of your mama and baba." All the humor fades from her ruddy face. "How are they doing?"

My impulse is to say they're fine, but I don't have the heart to lie—or the energy to tell the truth. So instead I ask, "Mrs. Hu, about Baba, has he . . . how long has he been drinking?"

Mrs. Hu sighs heavily, stalks over to her cart and sets the bag on top.

I watch her twist the top of the bag for a moment, but since she seems reluctant to say anything, I step closer and press on. "Is it all since Bao-bao died?"

She dips her head in a curt yes as she compresses the bag down, then lifts up the handles of her cart, readying to leave.

I put my hand on her arm to stop her. "I heard he wasn't doing well in school. Please tell me. How long has Bao-bao been—disappointing them?"

She heaves another sigh and gives me a long look before answering. "In his eleventh year, his grades started slipping. Your mama doubled her effort, got him extra tutoring. You know that's why they moved into the apartment next door to me, to save money. She first wanted to send him to a cram boarding school in Jinzhou. It costs almost three thousand yuan a month!"

My mouth falls open at the price. That's probably close to Mama's income. "How could they have even considered that?"

"They were counting on him for their future. A child is a parent's biggest investment." Mrs. Hu sighs and begins to pull her cart.

I put my hand on the bags to steady them and help her push the cart. The tires squeak loudly in the still night. "But why didn't they end up sending him there?"

"He talked them out of it. He said the expense would really hurt them. They would've had to take you out of your school. He said it wouldn't be fair to you."

My feet stop, and my hand slides off the pile, causing one of the bags to tumble off and spill several cans. I bend to pick everything up.

Bao-bao stood up for me? I never knew he thought about me at all, much less worried about my well-being and my future.

I feel Mrs. Hu's eyes on me I place the bag back on the cart, trying to find my tongue.

"So, they didn't make him go?" I ask.

"Your mama said he promised to bring his grades up on his own. He did, for a little while, but this last term, your mama found out he was skipping classes and lying to her about his rankings." Her voice is soft. "So many arguments. I could hear them through the wall. Mostly your baba, but your mama too, trying to reason with Bao-bao. Your baba had always liked to drink a couple of beers, a little baijiu, but these arguments with Bao-bao really"—she pauses—"affected him."

"Drinking more?"

"Yes. More and more, but nothing like what you saw when you got here. That started after the accident. That was the worst he's been. Has he been doing better since going home?"

I nod, though I'm not really sure. It's hard to tell from our brief phone calls. I'll have to remember to ask Gilbert to check on him when he has time.

"They put so much on that boy. But what else could they do?" Mrs. Hu brushes again at the gnats around our heads and looks down the empty street, where light pools from the streetlamps. Her lined face is drawn in the shadows. "It's the only way we know how to help them."

She's remembering her own dead son, I realize. My heart clenches, knowing that she has no one to take care of her and Mr. Hu in their old age.

"Na." Mrs. Hu's voice is low and choked. "No matter what you hear, your parents were just trying to help him the only way they knew how." Before I can think of a response, she grabs the handles of her cart again and pushes it down the alley toward Mr. Hu.

I leave too, hearing the distant clank of aluminum and the skitter of plastic as Mr. Hu tosses his found recyclables on the pavement.

No matter what you hear, your parents were just trying to help him. What did she mean by that? What more is there to hear?

22

After a few sessions of early morning teaching, I'm opening my eyes even before my alarm goes off. Each day, I slip out of the apartment, eagerly burst out into the street, and rush to the internet café, where even at 4:30 in the morning, at least half a dozen guys are glued to the monitors playing video games. Whenever I see them *click-click-click*ing, drinking Redbull, and eating spiced corned pig hooves, I can't help but imagine Bao-bao among them.

But I hurry to my station and quickly get immersed in my lesson. I'm filled with wonder that I'm talking with—no, *teaching*—a person on *the other side of the world!*

So far, all the students have been age nine and younger. Like Min predicted, I get to use my English because they often fall into their own language. And when they get restless, I speak to them in English, even making horrible mistakes on purpose so they can correct me. They really like that, and after they have a fit of laughing at me, I can steer them back to the Chinese.

The teaching job helps my time at the sorting facility go faster. All day, as I chuck metal into bins next to Mama, I run the lessons in my mind and invent ways to keep the students engaged.

Near the end of my second week, I'm surprised to see a high school guy on the screen when I connect.

"*Ni hao*?" I greet him.

He answers with surprisingly good tonal inflection. I introduce myself and ask him if he's eaten.

"My name is Ben," he answers. "Yes, I've eaten." He's not puzzled by the common greeting the way the younger kids have been.

"Your Chinese is very good," I tell him. "How much have you studied?"

"Four years so far. My teacher said I should try to . . . talk more before I go to China."

I tell him the word for conversation and ask about his plans to visit China. It takes a while to understand that he's going into his third year of high school and plans to study in China for eight weeks next summer. He's easily the most advanced student I've had, and rather than using the planned "ordering a meal" lesson, I ask him to tell me about himself.

He manages to tell me that he's sixteen, has a younger brother, and is half Chinese. His hair is dark brown and I only see a hint of his Chinese background in the shape of his eyes. I pepper him with more simple questions, his brother's name, what his parents do, what he likes to do outside of school. He plays guitar, soccer, and Fortnite, and hangs out with his friends. I suggest that he ask me questions.

"Do you have any brothers or sisters?" he asks.

"One brother," I answer, but instantly remember that I don't have one anymore.

"What's his name?"

I swallow. It would be too difficult to explain, so I just say, "Bao-bao."

"How old is he?"

"Seventeen." I grope for another question to change the subject.

Luckily, Ben does it for me. "What do you do for fun?" he asks.

The question catches me off guard. I'm not sure I like the casual conversation technique anymore, and the idea of going back to the suggested lesson crosses my mind, but I answer, "Well, I teach Chinese. I spend time with family. I go to college. I like to read. With friends I sing karaoke, play arcade games, take walks in the park."

There's no reason to tell him that I don't have much fun these days. He wouldn't understand if I told him the truth of my life. He seems so carefree, though he's just one year younger than Bao-bao.

"What are you studying?"

"Uh, English language," I lie again.

"Oh!" His face lights up and he switches to English. "What will you do with your degree?"

"I will teach," I answer in English.

"Nice!" He asks questions about my college. I make up all the answers, and soon I don't feel bad about lying. It's fun and we get caught up in the conversation, taking turns asking questions, switching between Chinese and English, helping each other find words.

Before I know it, Ben says his mother is calling him to dinner. The time in the corner of the screen shows 5:53. We've run over and I'm late. We sign off with a hurried goodbye. I pay up for the extra time that I've spent on the internet, rush out the door and check my phone, which I always turn off during a lesson.

Mama has texted me four times, each message more panicked. I start to run, dodging the other early risers who are now beginning to fill the sidewalks. The streetlights are still on, giving the gray dawn light a yellowish cast, the heat already rising from the pavement. Traffic isn't heavy, but plenty of cars and bikes weave in their lanes.

I'm halfway home when I see Mama ahead on the sidewalk.

Her face is white, wracked with anxiety, and I know she's looking for me. I streak toward her, and when she spots me, her expression transforms with utter relief. She grips my arms, and her eyes close for just a second, before they fly open and her face changes once again.

"Where have you been?!" Her fingers dig into my arms and vibrate with her anger. "What have you been doing?!"

"Teaching, Mama! I'm sorry, I lost track of the time." My voice is high-pitched and strained as I apologize. I hate that I made her worry, but I'm taken aback by her fury and suspicion.

"It's already past six! I didn't know where you were!" She looks at me accusingly. "I didn't think this was a good idea. You shouldn't be running around the city in the middle of the night." Her mouth opens and closes as if she wants to say more but she holds back.

"It's not the middle of night! It's morning, Mama!" I throw my arm out, gesturing to the traffic and people on the sidewalk. "It won't happen again. I'll set a timer next time. It was just such a good lesson. They gave me an older student today, more serious."

Mama's nostrils flare and her mouth closes up. It's clear that she doesn't want to hear any more. "We have to go right now to get the bus! You don't have time to eat, now!"

She lets go of me and storms off. I follow her. We pass our building and make it to the stop a few minutes before the bus arrives. Mama doesn't speak to me. I'm glad, because I'm annoyed by her overreaction, frustrated that I can't point it out. I breathe in and out heavily, trying to calm myself down.

Only after we slide into our seats and the bus is humming on the highway do I venture to apologize again. Mama faces the window, but she twists around briefly and gives a short nod to show that she's heard me.

"But Mama," I add, hating the tension between us, "the lesson was very productive. I think I helped the student very much. And when they give you older students, it means your ratings are good." I'm playing on her aspiration to see her children score well and it seems to work; the lines between her brows begin to ease. "The student was in high school, and he could carry a simple conversation. It was so much easier teaching him than the little ones. He was so serious about learning." I don't mention that he was fun to talk with. "And I got to use my English much more. My hope is that I'll keep getting more of the older students."

Although Mama doesn't make eye contact, I know she's listening. She no longer looks mad, but she doesn't smile either. She reaches into her bag, pulls out a cold steamed bun wrapped in paper, and hands it to me. I eat it while she goes back to staring out the window at the low-lying buildings and flat stretches of scrub on the outskirts of the city. When I'm done with the bun, I crumple the paper. She takes it from me and stuffs it back into her bag.

"We get paid next week," she says. "We'll pay Mrs. Hu with yours, and then we'll travel to Willow Tree for a few days. We can check on Ba and you can spend some time with Gilbert."

My mind gallops in different directions. I'll be happy to see Gilbert, and Baba too, though my stomach twists with anxiety over his condition. But I also wonder if the village's internet café will be open early enough for me to work with my students. "How many days?" I ask.

"Four."

"But will the boss allow it? I'll have only worked one month."

"If we promise to work one or two weeks overtime when we get back, I'm sure he'll agree."

My heart sinks. I've been going to bed as early as eight or nine every night. If I do overtime I won't get home until close to midnight. How will I be able to drag myself up at 3:45 in the mornings?

"He won't refuse," Ma snaps. "I want to do a tree burial for Bao-bao. He can't say no to that."

A tree burial. No, I suppose a person can't say no to that.

23

On the bus to Willow Tree Mama holds a stiff paper bag protectively in her lap, much like Baba held Bao-bao's urn. Inside the bag lies a white biodegradable urn box made of mulberry bark.

Mama ordered it online and showed it to me the other day when it arrived. She traced the embossed swirl pattern with her finger as she explained that cremations and tree burials are being encouraged by the government to make funerals more frugal and green—though really it's because cities are running out of space for cemeteries and memorial parks due to new construction that requires all the land. Even though it may not be traditional for parents to bury their son, Mama said that since the government is moving away from tradition, we can too.

I say out loud that I'm glad that we're doing this. Inside, I'm hoping that burying Bao-bao's ashes will give her a little more consolation. And Baba too.

"Mama, do you think that Baba will come back to Taiyuan with us?" I ask. Gilbert has reported that when he's seen Baba, he seems to be doing better.

"I don't know."

"It would be better for him to have something to do," I say. "To go back to work." I know it's helped her, although I don't say that.

"We'll see."

"If only he had something to do." I want her to encourage him to try, because it's not my place to do so. "It would help him to"—I almost say *forget*, but I know that's the wrong word—"get better."

"Maybe he'll stay in the village and help Nainai with the crops," Mama says flatly. She turns to the window.

I purse my lips doubtfully. He hasn't been doing anything so far, and I'm beginning to believe that Mama doesn't particularly care. It's almost as if she doesn't want him to come back.

"Mama, how did you and Baba meet?" The question comes out of nowhere, but it suddenly strikes me that I really know so little about them.

"In Taiyuan. Working in a toy factory." She throws the answer over her shoulder, keeping her face at the window.

"Well, how did you decide to get married?"

She shrugs. "We met. We were both country people working in the city. That's it."

"But what about love?"

"*Love is for teenagers, marriage is practical.* We liked each other enough to get married. Twenty-two years ago." Her gaze falls to the bag in her lap and she shakes her head slowly, as if in disbelief that so much time has passed. "We had you, and since you were a girl, we were allowed to try again. Then we had your brother. It turned out lucky for us." She sighs heavily. "For a while."

Her eyes move back to the dusty landscape and scrubs flying by, and I leave her alone.

Half an hour later, the bus pulls into the station of a small town. Mama and I stay put as a few people get off and others board. As we wait, Mama nudges me and points to a mural being painted on a white tiled building across the street.

GET MARRIED EARLY AND HAVE CHILDREN OF BETTER QUALITY! The slogan is painted in bold red above the oversized profiles of a married couple looking at each other. An open hand rests between their faces, holding two miniature children, a boy and a girl, who stand stalwartly against the backdrop of a rising sun.

I wrinkle my nose, but Mama smiles with amusement. "I wasn't sure at first about you getting married so soon, but more and more, I realize it's a good opportunity. A lot of girls now go for so much education and career that they become too picky. They think they can wait until later to marry, but then it might be too late."

She's parroting everything that the government wants us to believe, according to Min, and I wince to hear it come out of her mouth.

"If the government is relaxing the birth policy, it does make sense to get started earlier with the children." Mama smiles slyly. "Maybe in a few more years, the two-child policy will change to no policy at all, and you can have as many children as you want."

My face freezes. The realization that I might be pregnant this time next year hits me. And in less than two years there might be a child in my arms. A nervous patter begins in my chest, and I can only think to say, "But Mama, it's too expensive to have children!"

Mama nodded. "I know, I know. It's true. But don't worry about it." She strokes my arm and rests her hand on top of mine. "A grandchild would make all the difference to us. Your baba and I would feel like we've achieved something. We'll have done our duty."

Her small hand is light, though the palm is rough from work despite all the thick cream she slathers on every evening before bed. I'm not used to her touch, but I don't pull away.

◆ ◆ ◆

Gilbert meets us at the bus station. We're self-conscious around each other because Mama is there. We only grin at each other at first. Mama clasps Gilbert's arm as she greets him. Once she moves to walk ahead of us—obviously trying to give us privacy—Gilbert briefly squeezes my hand before he picks up our bags.

"Your ba wants to do the burial this afternoon," he tells me as we start for the house. "He and I have already dug the hole."

"Thanks for helping him. I'm so glad you've been here!" He really has been so helpful, checking in on Baba even though he's been busy with work. Just knowing he's here has lessened the worry. "Who's going to be at the funeral?"

"Just your family." He hesitates and studies me uneasily before going on. "Because of the *sad ending*, it has to be just family and all done quietly."

"Ah." A *sad ending* and a loss of face. "What about you? Can you come?"

"Oh, I'll be there. Your ba approves." His voice goes softer. "Since I'll be family soon?"

For the next moments, I can only hear my heart speeding in my chest. Already Gilbert has slipped into the role of son-in-law and solicitous husband. He's handsome and kind and hasn't pushed me to answer about getting married. With him beside me I can almost forget that rising dismay I've felt—the sense that work, marriage, babies were rushing up too fast. Marrying Gilbert is practical, but I can love him too. I already do. I duck my head in a nod, confirming our engagement.

Gilbert's grin grows wider, and he breathes out an exaggerated sigh. "I'm so glad that's settled!"

24

In the afternoon Mama, Nainai, Gilbert and I, all clad in white shirts, set out for the hike to our family burial plot. Baba has gone ahead.

He and Mama argued about the burial when we arrived at the house earlier. He didn't want her to pour Bao-bao's ashes into the box, didn't want to bury him, but Mama took the urn from the windowsill and hissed that he was her son too, and she would have his soul rest. Baba spun on his heel and left the house, but not before he grabbed the bottle of baijiu.

Now, the brown hills and green terraced fields are scorching hot, the sky big and open overhead. We pass fields of bright yellow rapeseed, castor bean, and tall sunflowers with their heads as large as ours that seem to rotate and watch us as we tread single file up the path. Ahead, at the top of a hill, I see the tablets marking our ancestors' graves in the shade of three jujube trees. I've been there many times before on Tomb-Sweeping Days, and during the Spring Festival break when we always come to show our respect. But as we mount the hill, I don't see any sign of Baba.

I'm surprised when Gilbert leads us past the family

graves, but when Mama and Nainai don't even slow their steps, I'm almost sure that this must be the custom of a *sad ending*: Bao-bao must be separated from the rest of the family.

We go down the other side of the hill and around another bend before I finally see Baba standing beneath a straggly pear tree. As we get closer, I see the neat square hole he and Gilbert have dug beneath it. The upturned dirt is piled up next to it. Baba sways on his feet, staring into the small pit, his face cloudy with emotions. He doesn't acknowledge our arrival. The bottle of baijiu is slipped in his pants pocket, so I can't see how much he's drunk.

I stand back a little with Gilbert while Mama places the biodegradable box into the hole. She backs away to stand next to Nainai, their heads bent down in their private pain. Baba glowers at the white box. His bitter expression makes my stomach contract. He seems to be on the verge of another breakdown or at least an outburst.

I bite my lips, holding back my own feelings. I *am* sorry about Bao-bao's death now. But we didn't know each other as a brother and sister should, and I'll never have the chance to know him like Min and Wei did, so I still find myself more moved by my family's agony, by the trouble his death has caused, than by Bao-bao's death itself.

I have such an awful uneasiness rising in my chest, I can't think about him here. I reach for Gilbert's hand hanging beside mine. He grips it hard and gives me a comforting look. His kindness almost makes me cry, and I lightly lean my shoulder against his arm.

I'm anxious for the burial to be finished. I have a tiny hope that maybe Mama and Baba can start to move on after it's done.

I'm glad when Gilbert lets go of my hand, takes up the shovel leaning against the tree, and edges around Mama and Nainai to fill in the hole.

Baba moves like lightning, seizing the shovel, breaking the silence. "I'm his father! I'll do it myself!"

Gilbert releases the shovel and steps back beside me. We all watch as Baba spades the dirt. The only sounds are of the shovel cutting into the earth, the dirt showering the box, and Baba huffing. His movements are lurching, and the soil doesn't always make it into the hole. Almost immediately he's drenched in sweat, and I can smell the alcohol coming out of his pores.

Mama closes her eyes. Her face is white as marble. I hold my breath against a dreadful sense of foreboding, but Baba manages to get it done. He throws the shovel down and buckles to his knees and pats the earth tight. Tracks of tears are now running down his face.

Mama kneels down. She fishes inside the bag she brought, pulling out Bao-bao's glasses, his math book, and some of his old certificates rolled up and tied with a ribbon. She lays them out on the grave with a defiant set to her jaw.

It's all very peculiar, not like the days-long funeral we had for Yeye when I was very small with the coffin and the wake, the crowded meal in the courtyard for all the villagers, the long funeral procession and the noise of wailing echoing in the hills. Even our yearly visits to Yeye's grave are almost festive, with food laid out, fireworks, and the burning of paper money and goods.

I look at Baba and Mama, their wet faces swollen and blotchy. Before this summer, I never saw them fight, other than minor squabbles about Baba getting too rowdy during the holidays, Mama being too bossy, or some other small complaint, always followed by good-natured headshakes and suppressed laughs. Now, they don't even acknowledge each other, much less try to comfort each other. All their affection seems to be gone.

The sun is blazing down on my black hair. I have no tears for Bao-bao, or for Baba and Mama. I'm so tired of the heaviness that I just want all this be over. I want to go back to the house, back to the city, back to college, which starts in just another week. I can't help thinking of the days when I had time to read, play with makeup, and huddle at Xioawen's laptop watching shows. But those times are already like an old memory, and I know I can't go back there. My heart pounds, longing to be away from all this, to be gone.

Gilbert takes my hand once more. His grip is firm and reassuring. I clutch tightly as if he's the only thing preventing me from hurtling off into oblivion. Nainai glances back at us. I see her look down at my white-knuckled hand intertwined with Gilbert's before her sad eyes run up to my face. She studies me with what looks like pity, and after a long moment she gestures with her head for Gilbert and me to go back.

I don't hesitate. Gratefully, I tug on his hand, and we leave. Mama and Baba don't pay any attention to us.

We're up the hill, past the family plots and heading back down the other side before I can breathe.

"That was rough. Are you okay?" Gilbert says softly.

I nod curtly and keep my head down. I sense Gilbert is casting about for more sympathetic remarks.

"When do you have to leave?" I say to head off any more talk about the burial. Gilbert already explained that he has a work conference tomorrow in Changyu Township about an hour away. There's no early morning bus on Sunday, so he has to stay in a hotel there tonight.

"I should go get my things together now. The bus leaves at 4:30. I'm so sorry that this meeting is tomorrow of all weekends."

"It's okay, you can't help it." I try to keep the heaviness out of my voice.

He eyes me with a mix of sorrow and guilt. "Maybe I should stay. Skip the meeting."

"You can't miss the meeting. You just started your job a few weeks ago. I'll be all right."

"I'll be back after lunch tomorrow. And we'll also have Monday evening to see each other when I get home from work."

He's trying to make me feel better, and I smile to let him know that I understand. It touches me that he's sorry about leaving me alone here, missing our time together.

We walk silently for a few moments before he says, "Oh, did you ask your English language boss about changing teaching times?" He suggested this a few days ago after I asked him to check when the village internet café was open.

"Yes. She said she'll give me students and eight and nine at night for the next three days, though it means I'm back to teaching the younger kids."

"Good! The café is open until eleven. The other thing is that they only have six computers so you'd better get there early. Will your parents mind you being out so late?"

I shrug. I'm not sure if they'll fret over me or if they won't even notice that I'm gone. Both scenarios depress me. "Do you mind if I tell them that I'm with you?"

"Of course not." He's quick to answer, and with such understanding as to why I have to lie that the tears that I've been suppressing all day come to my eyes. I turn away, surprised and embarrassed by them.

"Oh no. Come here!" Gilbert pulls me close and wraps me in his arms. I lean against him and for the next moments, there's only his solid warmth as everything else falls away.

25

After a late breakfast on Sunday, Mama goes out to Bao-bao's grave. Baba doesn't get up until after she leaves in the late morning. He staggers out of his room, still wearing the clothes he wore yesterday, and guzzles a jar of cooled tea that Nainai hands him. His eyes rove the room, wavering as they go from me—cross-legged on the kang reading *Jane Eyre*—to the empty urn on the windowsill, to the folded blankets and pillow on the other end of the kang where Mama slept last night.

"Where's your ma?" Baba sounds hoarse, garbled.

"She went to Bao-bao," I answer.

Baba looks out the window and blinks, slow as a turtle, before he squats onto a stool. Nainai sets down a bowl of millet porridge in front of him. Baba takes up the spoon and begins to eat, staring dully at the middle distance in front of him.

Nainai and I glance at each other before she starts to clean up. She works without her usual brisk clatter, doing her best to be unobtrusive. I hide behind my book, trying to travel back to the Moor House with Jane, but the air in the room is tense, strained, and although I can read the words in English, I can't get my mind to decode their meaning.

I wonder if the funeral was a good idea. Over the past several weeks, Baba was sounding better each time I talked to him on the phone, but now, although he's not crying and sloppy drunk as he was at the start of the summer, his brooding is like a brewing storm. He slurps down his porridge noisily, pushes the bowl aside and lurches to the window. His fingers run over Bao-bao's urn, his thumb stopping to rub the gray oval where Bao-bao's photo had never been affixed. With his back to me I can't see his expression, but I hold my breath.

His head rises, and I know he's looking out the window again. He lists to one side as he stands there, and I can see that he's lost weight from the way his pants sag low on his hips. I grip my book, expecting him to lose his balance, or to blow up, but he only turns, stumbles back to his room and slams the door.

Nainai sighs and I put my book down. It's useless trying to read. I wish that Gilbert was here.

Nainai looks at my book, splayed open and facedown on my bed. "You always like to study, I know. But you'll see, soon you'll have a family and you'll be so busy raising a little one." She pulls a one-sided smile.

I can't help but wince. She's trying to make me feel better about not going back to college, but weirdly, her sympathy makes me feel worse. I really am excited about marrying Gilbert.

"It's terrible that your Gilbert had to work today! Overtime on Sunday!"

"It was just for the morning. He'll be home after lunch."

"These companies, they expect too much!" She clicks her tongue. "But he has to go. It's the only way to climb up. At least he's not labor. He's done well with his college, eh?"

I grin, proud for him.

"Yes, we're lucky with Gilbert! He's already doing better than his parents, or yours. It's a shame your mama picked this weekend, when he has to work, for you two to come home." She glances at the clock over the stove. "The bus going west leaves at 10:30. Changyu Township's only about an hour away. You should take the bus over and meet him in town. Then you can ride home together. You two need to spend time together. Have to get to know each other better! That's more important now than reading that book."

It's a great idea. I'm ready to leap for the extra hour with Gilbert, but my eyes slide uneasily to Baba's door.

Nainai lowers her voice. "Don't worry. You go. He and your mama would want you to."

Gratefully, I gather up my book and purse, and slip on my shoes. I hurry to leave before Mama returns or Baba comes out of his room. They may be pleased for me to spend time with Gilbert, but it's nice to go without having to report my movements.

I feel as if I've been set free, and I'm eager to meet up with Gilbert. Although I intended to pick up with *Jane Eyre* on the bus, I find it hard to keep my mind on the words. My rural middle school education makes reading in English slow going, despite my independent study. I have to hold back from flipping to the Chinese like Min did.

I finally give up and gaze out the window. The low brown mountains seem to roll on and on endlessly except where they've been terraced into fields or where the hillsides have crumbled away, as if a giant hand grabbed a ridge and dragged its fingers down the hillside. I remember the violent dust storms of winter and the occasional downpours that would shift a stream or damage the fields, but from the long view, the hills were always still there, ceaselessly undulating, so much the same.

Changyu Township is much like Willow Tree Village, though it sprawls out with more streets. At first I consider waiting for Gilbert at the bus station, but when the ticket seller asks me what I'm doing, I explain about the conference. He tells me the Friendship Hotel, two streets over, is the only place large enough to hold that kind of meeting.

When I get there, I see that the hotel is an old building, only two floors and shabby. There is no one in the small lobby, not even a clerk. An old-fashioned bell sits on the wooden counter and I mash it with my finger. Eventually a woman comes out, dragging a bucket with her, and moves to stand behind the counter. I ask her where the coal conference is being held.

She frowns. "No conference here."

I thought Gilbert called it a conference, but maybe I misunderstood the size of the gathering. "Well, maybe it's just a meeting. Don't you have a big room where a meeting might take place?"

"The banquet hall, through those doors." She points to the double doors, slightly ajar, that face the counter. I step over and peer in. The room has garish red carpeting and vinyl black dining chairs at the half dozen round tables. Only one man, eating alone, is seated at a table in the back.

"No meeting, but you can get lunch now," the housekeeper-clerk says behind me.

I'm puzzled, wondering if there's another meeting space in town, but the ticket seller at the bus station said this was the only hotel. "Do you have a Liang Huan staying here?"

"Room 8." She doesn't have to look it up, just jabs a finger toward the open door leading to the stairs. "Second floor."

I go up, noting how odd it was that she knew Gilbert's room right off, but with the almost empty dining room and lobby the hotel has an unoccupied atmosphere, so I suppose there are only so many guests. I wonder if the meeting ended early. Although the housekeeper-clerk surely would have mentioned it.

Room 8 is at the end of the hall. The walls are thin enough that I hear voices and low laughter just before I rap on the door.

The voices stop. No one answers, so I knock again.

I hear noises inside, the creak of a bed, footsteps muffled by carpet, a door shut within. My skin prickles over.

"Who is it?"

"Gilbert? It's Na!"

"Na!"

He doesn't come to the door right away, and I hear more flurried noise inside, fast footsteps padding around the room. More than just two feet. A thrumming starts inside my head. Minutes seem to pass as my eyes lock on the doorknob, but I don't allow a clear thought to form in my mind. By the time the knob turns, my neck and face are mottled with hot splotches.

Gilbert, pushing up his glasses, swings the door open. "Na, what are you doing here?"

I look past him. Guo-Rong sits hunched on the end of one of the two beds, his hand raking back his thick hair. I almost laugh with relief. Gilbert hadn't mentioned that Guo-Rong was going to be at the conference as well.

"You remember Guo-Rong from school?" Gilbert gestures toward him.

"Of course." I'm smiling, mostly to myself as the heat in my face begins to dissipate.

Guo-Rong stands and inclines his head at me. "Well, I better get back to the conference." He puts a hand up in a curt wave.

Gilbert and I start to move out of the doorway to let him pass, but Guo-Rong abruptly stops and turns back to the room. He's wearing slippers, and as he shucks them off, I see they're the cheap hotel issue.

A funny feeling comes over me as he slips his bare feet into his shoes, acting as if he always puts his shoes on without socks. I notice then that he's wearing black jeans, a T-shirt. He pats his pockets as if searching for something, while his eyes dart around until he locates his phone on the bedside table.

Blood roars in my ears again, and I watch him, as if in slow motion, go around the bed, pick up his phone from the bedside table, and pocket it.

"I'll see you," Guo-Rong mutters to Gilbert as he leaves.

My mouth is dry, and Gilbert is talking to me, but I don't hear his words. One bed is rumpled, with sheets and a blanket tossed on the floor. Two overnight bags with clothes spilling out of them sit on the other bed, which is otherwise neatly made with its tan bedspread. Unused.

"Na!" Gilbert puts his hands on my shoulders and spins me to him. "What are you doing here? Is everything okay?" He leans toward me, concern overtaking the guilt and nervousness on his face. "What is it? Why didn't you call me to tell me you were coming?"

I step back, pulling out of his grasp, and take in his wrinkled shirt and loose workout shorts, knowing they were hastily thrown on. My stomach is turning sour, acid pooling. I swallow. "The hotel seems awfully empty for a conference."

"It ended early," Gilbert says. His eyes are unnaturally rounded.

I shake my head slowly. "Please don't."

He drops down to the bed, his hands covering his face. His shirt gapes open at the collar where the top three buttons haven't been fastened. *Your smooth chest against mine.*

I'm waiting for him to tell me, but already I know. I spin on my heel and bolt out of the room.

26

The bus home won't leave for another hour, and I don't want to run into Gilbert or Guo-Rong at the station. There's a small restaurant a few doors away, so I slink in and take a seat in the back of the room. The other diners, two old men, are already eating so the waitress comes to me right away and asks me what I want. I order a Coke, and when she brings it, I take a sip and the warm liquid fizzes down my throat. She hovers over me waiting for me to order food. I ask for a bowl of noodles though I can't possibly eat anything.

When the waitress goes back to the kitchen I close my eyes and listen to the noise of chopping, the men talking, the clinking of their chopsticks against their bowls. I try not to think, not to let the reality seep into my brain. But the truth is screaming at me.

Gilbert is *gay*. He and Guo-Rong are gay . . . together.

I shudder, not even understanding what that really means. I've never known anyone who was gay. I've heard mention of it in episodes of some American shows and movies, and a few sly allusions to it in college, but here in the countryside, it's unspeakable—considered unnatural, maybe even a mental disorder. Images of the two of them together flicker through my mind: rumpled beds, bare chests, kissing. I shut my eyes hard trying to drive them out of my head.

And Gilbert tried to trick me into marrying him! The sudden realization hits me. I've been a fool. I *am* such a fool.

My ears burn with humiliation, and my fists are clenched on *Jane Eyre* in my lap. Somehow the book wasn't lost when I fled the hotel. The irony is glaring. Horrible secrets. Deceit. I should have nicknamed Gilbert Mr. Rochester. Only Gilbert doesn't love me like Mr. Rochester loved Jane. He isn't desperate to marry me despite the secret he has locked up. He wanted to marry me specifically to keep his secret hidden away.

And I almost fell for it. Another wave of humiliation courses over me.

I curse Gilbert with every dirty name I've ever heard. Angry tears are just below the surface, and I fight to keep them from seeping out.

The noodles arrive. I keep my head bent so the waitress can't see my face, but she stands there with a hand on her hip. I pick up my chopsticks and bring some noodles to my mouth, chewing, chewing, until she's satisfied that I'm eating and goes away. The noodles are slippery in my mouth, salty as tears. I force myself to swallow them.

I check the time on my phone. I'm desperate to be on the bus, to leave, though it suddenly occurs to me that Gilbert will probably be riding home on the same bus. And when I get home, I'll have to tell my parents and Nainai . . . something. What can I possibly say?

The metal bell hanging on the door handle chimes. I see Gilbert peer in and spot me right away. He comes inside, crossing over to my table. My seat scrapes back as I jump up, ready to run out.

He catches my arm before I can move around the table. "Na, please wait."

I jerk my arm back. *Jane Eyre* flies out of my hand and hits the floor.

"Please, Na," he whispers and glances around the room. The two old men are twisting around to look our way, and the waitress stands in the kitchen doorway craning her neck to listen.

I glare at her until she returns to the kitchen. After a moment I sit back down. Gilbert picks up my book and sets it on the table before taking the chair beside me and dropping his overnight bag. I can't even look at him.

"Na." He leans in to keep his voice low. "I'm sorry. I don't know what to say."

The fury inside me is boiling. I want to grab the Coke and fling it at his head. Another stream of curses runs through my mind, but I hold back. He doesn't deserve my breath.

"Please. I'm sorry I brought you into this," he says. "I thought it would help both of us."

"What do you mean?" I demand, further enraged by that excuse. "How were *you* helping *me*? You wanted to use me to cover your—"

"Shhh!" Gilbert glances around and tensely smiles at the men who are looking our way again.

One of them mutters, "Lovers' quarrel," before the clattering of their chopsticks resumes.

"You—well, your family, I mean . . . Yes, it's true, I deceived you." He brings his arms onto the table and leans forward again. "But your family was in such a bad situation. My ma and my nainai always had it in their minds that maybe we would get married. They teased me about it. Both of us. You remember!

175

And you know how everyone worries about their son not being able to find a wife, especially if you're from the countryside."

His words are measured, reasonable, but with a pleading undercurrent.

"When your brother died, Nainai thought it would be a good time to propose. She and my parents are so afraid I won't be able to find a wife since I've gotten stuck with a job out here. And she said marriage might help your family since your brother . . . had such a *sad ending.*"

"You mean everyone considers my family cursed, so no one else will marry me?" I hiss.

"You and I both know that it's shit. But my family kept pressing me. Na, I've always liked you. We've always gotten along. I thought . . . both our parents would get what they wanted. Your nainai and your parents were really suffering, and you've said yourself how they've come out of it some since I proposed. I didn't think it through. I should've told you the whole truth, asked you differently. But you can't imagine how it is to be . . . like this." He plops back against his chair and folds his arms across his body.

In spite of myself, I feel a tiny speck of sympathy for him. I know in my bones what's expected of a son, a singleton, the kind of pressure put on him to achieve, marry, have a child. Being gay would never be acceptable for Gilbert. But that's no excuse for how he's treated me. "What about me? I would have been a *gay wife!*"

"I would have tried to be a good husband. I can't change who I'm attracted to, but that doesn't mean I can't . . ." Gilbert hesitates and swallows nervously. "What I'm trying to say is— we still could've had a baby."

I shrink back, bewildered that he's still pushing for marriage.

"That look on your face." Gilbert draws away further and slumps back in his chair, disappointed. "I thought about telling you before I suggested we get married, but that look on your face, that's why I didn't. You can't possibly understand. I don't choose to be like this!"

He's trying to turn it on me. "But you tried to trick me! If I married you then I would've given up my chance to have a *real* husband."

"You're working in that plant! Who are you going to meet there? A laborer? With your brother gone and with all the propaganda the government puts out, your parents would have been pressuring you to marry soon anyway. But you're only just about to turn twenty. We could marry for a few years, have a child, then get a divorce. You'd still be young enough to get married again."

I shake my head, more from instinct than because I'm actually absorbing what he's suggesting.

"It would work, Na. All our parents care about is getting a grandchild. How many times do you hear *Of the three major violations of filial piety, not producing a successor is the greatest?* I'm so sick of that talk!" His eyes roll as his hands rake through his hair.

Of course I've heard that saying. It's still practically Confucius's most popular line. But I bite my lips, refusing to concede to anything he has to say.

"If we had a kid, you would've done your duty. And if we divorced, our parents would get over it because it's gotten so common now. Then you can take your time finding the right person to marry again."

He hunches forward and says more softly, "I still think it's a good idea for us to get married, despite . . . everything.

People do it. It's called a *mutual help marriage*." He reaches for my hand.

I try to pull away, but he holds on. "Na, listen. Your parents have taken you out of school! You're working in that awful plant when you're way too smart for that. Maybe you'll meet someone in a better position who wants you for a nice, submissive wife, mother, and daughter-in-law. Is that what you want? I know I'm not a great prize for you, and you can probably find a better husband, but I promise I'll help you somehow. You want to go back to school, right? I promise I'll figure something out. I'm not going to stay out here in the countryside forever, but while we're here, you can study for the gaokao."

My pulse skips a beat.

"We'll eventually move to a city, and I don't mean just Taiyuan, but a first-tier city like Beijing or Shanghai, or wherever you get accepted to college. You'll study English, get a degree, like you've always wanted."

I don't remember ever telling Gilbert that I wanted to study English at college. Hearing him mention it as if it's the most natural thing in the world makes me want to cry.

"Out here all anyone cares about is that you get married and have a kid. It'll be different in the city." He releases my hand and picks at the strip of vinyl that wraps the table's edge.

"And what about Guo-Rong?" I say it accusingly. I'm not ready to stop being angry.

He colors again and shifts his eyes away before they jump back to me. "I won't see him anymore. I'll put that all aside while we're married. We'll give our parents a child. They'll be happy. And we'll be happy in the city. Please just think about it."

Despite myself, I can feel my anger cooling. Gilbert's pleading and rationalizations have calmed me down, but I don't want him to know it. I keep tight-lipped. He asks if I'm going to eat the noodles, and I flick my hand at him to take them.

When he's done eating, we go to the bus station and board the bus. I don't sit with him, but choose the empty seat across the aisle. He smiles at me sadly and twists to rest his head on the plate window, staring up at the sky. He looks lost and miserable.

That prick of sympathy is back. It was horrible of him to deceive me, but I can understand why he was afraid to tell me the truth. And I suppose he really can't help being gay.

Gay! I'm still stunned. My mind is in turmoil. I feel so stupid and ignorant, and I want to cover those feelings with outrage. And yet . . . I think about how he stuck up for me so I could go to school. The copy of *Anne of Green Gables* he gave me. All our long bus rides over the years. He's still the kind and thoughtful Gilbert I've known all my life.

I glance over to him again, the back of his head to me. All those long bus rides, and he couldn't even tell me.

Probably because he knew how I'd react. Maybe I'm no different than our neighbors who've judged us and shunned us in the wake of Bao-bao's death. Afraid of what I can't explain, what I've been raised to fear.

I don't know. It's all too fresh to sort out. But I do believe that Gilbert didn't choose to be gay, and that he wants to do the right thing.

He thinks that I can't understand, but on some level I do. At least the part about obligations to the family. *Of all behavior, filial piety comes first.* The thought of telling my parents that the marriage is off fills me with dread.

My mind drifts to what Gilbert said about *mutual help.* I consider what marrying Gilbert offers me beyond satisfying— no, *pleasing*—my parents.

Could it really be possible for me to take the gaokao? Go to college as an English major? Could I trust Gilbert to help me and make it all work out?

Could I bear to wait on him to advance and move us to the city, depend on him for my turn to do something?

I look at him again from the sides of my eyes. His head is bent forward now. He looks grim, with his jaw clenched. My chest is suddenly achy as I realize he never loved me, and won't ever love me as a woman. I'm not sure any amount of security, any kind of potential for a brighter future, will compensate for that.

27

Willow Tree is sleepy with the heat of the afternoon. The shops are mostly shuttered, and even the children who are out seem to hover in the shade of the buildings and alleys while they listlessly scratch at the ground with sticks. Gilbert and I, several feet between us, plod down the main street and through the twisty lanes in the direction of our homes. I'm thick-headed, moving like a dreamwalker.

Out of the corner of my eye, I see Gilbert's mouth part a few times as if he wants to say something, but I'm glad he doesn't apologize or press his case any further. He made his case very clearly and to hear it again would only irritate me.

The question to marry or not marry is hanging thick in the air between us, but unlike when Gilbert first proposed, this time there is no giddiness. My feet itch to pull away from Gilbert, but I trudge slowly, not wanting to get home.

Eventually I peel off at my family's lane with a curt twitch of my head, not even meeting his eyes. As I'm about to go around the curve Gilbert shouts, "Na!"

I turn to see that he has stopped in the lane with his duffle in hand.

"I'll be a good husband," he calls out. "We can make it

work. *Love is for teenagers, marriage is practical.*"

The same saying Mama used. *Practical.* If anything, I've always been practical.

I start to walk away, but then I spin back around.

Gilbert's still standing there. His face lights up, but I shake my head. "It's not going to happen, Gilbert. I'm not going to marry you."

"Na—"

"Don't," I say gently, firmly. I'm sorry for him, sorry for myself, but there's nothing more to say. Not right now.

❖❖❖

No one is home when I return. The yaodong is mercifully still, and I'm relieved not to have to face Mama and Nainai's curious looks and questions. Everyone is probably at the grave. I don't know how I'm going to tell them.

I drop my purse and my book on the kang. The bonneted Jane stares up at me from the book cover, the hulking estate of Thornfield looming behind her. Min said the novel might be helpful in my situation. Mr. Rochester with his secret? Practical St. John?

But this is no romantic novel, and I'm not an orphan with the freedom to make my own choices. It's not easy to throw off a lifetime—generations really—of ingrained duty to one's family. Even Min admitted that. Someone has always told me what to do, and that makes me feel both childish and weary-old at once.

I grab the book and throw it across the room. It makes a satisfying smack against the wall and tumbles down on Bao-bao's bags.

I climb up on the kang near the window and fold my legs up to my chest. Bao-bao's urn isn't in its usual place on the sill. I wonder if Baba has taken it with him to Bao-bao's grave.

My poor brother. All those years I was so jealous of him. I imagined he was Mama's and Baba's spoiled *little emperor.* Everyone, even Nainai, pinned the whole family's aspirations on him. He was supposed to study all the time, make a perfect grade on the gaokao, become an engineer, get a job, buy a house, buy a car, get married, have a child, and take care of Mama and Baba in their old age.

I never fully understood the depth of responsibility that went along with all that attention. Bao-bao actually spared me from it. I was at school, free from daily scrutiny and expectations, enjoying myself, yet simmering with resentment about the special treatment he was getting. He was broken by it, and I wonder now if I could have somehow helped him.

No matter what you hear, your parents were just trying to help him. Mrs. Hu's remark comes back to me. I still don't know what she meant by that.

I go to Bao-bao's bags and unzip the one with his books. His zodiac series is still wedged between two of them, and I pull the drawings out, flipping through them slowly. The detail and exquisite shading astound me all over again, but it breaks me up inside that he had to keep all this hidden away.

The ruined drawings are here as well. When I first found them I imagined Bao-bao ripped them up in a fit of frustration, but considering what Min and Wei told me, I suppose now that Baba must have found them and tried to destroy them. *Just trying to help him.*

I come to the small red painting of Ai Weiwei's quote that I placed with Bao-bao's art. *Freedom is a strange thing.*

Once you've experienced it, it remains in your heart, and no one can take it away.

Did Bao-bao ever really feel freedom? He had his sports, video games, friends, and drawing, but he had to hide them from our parents even as he resisted their narrow plans for him. Eventually, he gave up.

At his grave, Mama and Baba laid out his school things—his math book and certificates. But that wasn't really Bao-bao. That was just how they wanted to see him, how they wanted him to be. I huff, seeing how it's the same for Gilbert, for me; all of us caught in our parents' expectations. I pull my braid around and twist it, heartsick for all of us and outraged for Bao-bao, who even in death can't be himself.

These drawings should be what lie on his grave. Or maybe they should even be burned and sent up to him. Impulsively, I roll up the drawings, pull the elastic band from the tail of my hair, and slip it around them.

At the stove, I'm rooting around for matches when I hear scuffling footsteps in the courtyard. Nainai comes running in.

"Na!" she huffs as she lunges toward me. "You're here!" She drops down onto a stool while hanging on my arm. Her face is damp with sweat and tears, twisted in distress.

"Nainai! What's wrong?"

She's trying to catch her breath. "Your ba—your ma!" She pushes me in the direction of the door. "Go—the grave!" is all that she can get out.

I don't want to leave her like this, but she thrusts her hand fiercely toward the door. I run out and fly down the path toward the grave with a growing dread. Has Baba passed out? Or is it Mama this time? My feet kick up the dirt, the grains dusting my ankles.

Well before I get there, I hear the shouting. It's Baba. And I'm sure he's drunk.

When I round the bend, I stop with a stitch in my side, heaving for air in the thick heat. I see down the hill that Baba's kneeling at the grave while Mama stands over him shrieking.

"Go away!" he roars at Mama. He reaches backward and pushes at her legs before he turns back to Bao-bao's grave and plows into the dirt with his hands.

I go cold when I notice the cloisonné urn with the lid removed on the ground beside him, and Mama screams, "Let him be!"

He's digging up Bao-bao's ashes.

Mama's crying. Her hands are fisted up near her shoulders. As she leans in to yell at Baba to stop, I'm afraid she's going to pummel him. He ignores her and keeps digging.

"Leave him alone!" Mama drops down and pushes the dirt back in. I'm frozen in place as my parents are caught in a whirl of dirt circling in and out of the hole, until Mama finally lunges at Baba and shoves him. Baba topples over, bumping the urn, but he doggedly clambers back onto his knees and resumes digging. He slurs, "Can't let him disappear . . . turn to dust . . . not right!"

"Stop it! Stop it. Leave him alone. You have no right. You did this! You killed him! You killed my boy!"

"Mama! Don't say that!" I dart down the hill, appalled that she would blame Baba like this when he blames himself already. "It's not his fault!"

"Not his fault!" Mama turns on me with wild rage. "He did this! He did it. With his own hands! He hit my boy and knocked the life out of him."

"No, Mama! No!" I grab her by the shoulders, furious that

she's torturing Ba like this. "Bao-bao did it to himself. Bao-bao ate rat poison."

"No!" She twists out of my grip and turns away, her shoulders shuddering as she sobs. For a moment she seems to be calming down, but suddenly she spins back around. "It wasn't the poison that killed him," she screams. "Ba hit him. His head smacked the bedstead, and Baba just left him."

"No, Mama!" I shake my head. "Mrs. Hu told me it was rat poison!"

"We put the poison there! Put it in his mouth, in his hands, to cover up that your ba killed him!" She doubles over and puts her face in her hands.

She's wailing, and the noise becomes a distant ringing in my ears as I stare at her with a great rising dread. It can't be true. I don't believe it. I look to Baba, wanting him to deny it. He has stopped digging and just sits there, shaking. His fists are mashed to his chest, covered in dirt.

"Baba!"

He rocks back and forth.

"Ba!" A great lump pushes up into my throat.

Tears stream down his face, making a smeary mess. He begins to mumble. I lean forward to make out what he's saying.

"I did it. I killed my boy. I did it."

My eyes go back and forth between the two of them. "But it was an accident?" My voice cracks, sounding hollow.

Mama is still hunched over on her knees. Her hands now clamp over her mouth, and she gazes wretchedly into the excavated grave.

Baba drops his hands into his lap, muttering on and on, "I did it. I did it." With his eyes closed and his face streaked with dirt, he looks dead himself.

I feel myself go white. Mama, Baba, the tree, the cloisonné urn, and the dirt spiral around me. I back away, stunned and horrified.

The next thing I know I'm scrambling down the path toward home. From out of nowhere Nainai appears, reaching her arms out as if to stop me. But I don't stop. I skirt a wide arc out of her grasp and keep going. Briefly, I wonder if she knows the truth, but I smudge the question out of my mind. It doesn't matter, I don't want to know.

I burst into the yaodong and stand, panting, sweat trickling down my back. The walls, covered in peeling newspaper and our old family photos, close in on me. My eyes flit around the curved room, from Nainai's chair, to the stove where I cooked for Nainai and me, to the table where Bao-bao and I did our homework.

Bao-bao's drawings are fanned out on the kang. I left them rolled up when Nainai sent me out to Baba and Mama. She must've opened them. What she must've thought . . .

I see the Ai Weiwei quote is lying top and center, and suddenly, I know what I'm going to do.

28

I sit in the very first seat behind the driver, my eyes fixed straight ahead over his shoulder and through the windshield, as if the force of my gaze will spur the bus to eat the asphalt even faster.

The bus grinds in and out of little towns. People climb on and off the bus, but I take no notice of them. At times I'm aware of a dull hum in my ear as if my brain is trying to shirr itself together after being ruptured into thousands of pieces.

A few times, when my phone dings with a text, I see in my mind Mama screaming and Baba digging up the grave, but I don't look at the messages. Instead I swiftly shake my head until the images blur away with the passing landscape and the miles of road between us.

Only when the sun begins its slow setting and the lanes of the highway begin to double, then triple, do I force myself to organize my thoughts. I check the time on my phone. The first thing I have to do is to get to an internet café. Now more than ever I can't afford to miss my teaching sessions, because it's the only sure thing I have at the moment.

When the bus pulls into Taiyuan, I go straight to my regular café, with just enough time to text Min and tell her I need to see her when I finish here. I see the texts from Mama, but I don't read them and I don't call her. My hair, freed from its band, has messily come undone and sticks to my damp neck. I smooth it back as best I can while I wait for a response from Min.

She doesn't answer before I have to sign on with my students. I'm distracted while I teach, glancing repeatedly at my phone beside my desk even though I've shut it off. Somehow I manage to fix a smile on my face and chatter to my students over the next two hours, though a riot of urgent plans and suppressed thoughts has begun to bounce in the back of my mind.

For the first time, I'm glad when the lessons are done. It's after 10:00 p.m. Min has answered that she and Wei are going to put up her exhibit in the park, and I can meet her there. The day has been so jarring, so disturbing and depleting, I'm surprised by the blip of cheer that passes through me, knowing that I'll get to see her installation before I go.

My hand slips down to grasp my travel bag. That Wei is with Min is another stroke of luck, because I intend to sell Bao-bao's designs to him. I need money if I'm going to go back to Linfen, to finish my degree in coal technology.

If I can just get enough for the first month's tuition, I'll manage after that. I plan to beg Min's friend for more online teaching sessions, and if that doesn't cover me, I'll find cleaning work or wash dishes at a restaurant. But for now I need to get that first 350 yuan, and after I sell Bao-bao's designs, I'm hoping I can borrow the rest from Min. I know it's a lot to ask of her, we've only known each other for a short time, but I'm sure she'll want to support what I'm doing.

Coal technology may not be as ambitious as studying for the gaokao or getting an English degree. But it's a first step, and for now, like Min said, it's enough to be *riding the donkey to find a horse.*

A sign at the entrance states that the park closes at nine, yet a few lampposts still light the main promenade. I peer down the paved winding walkway. The park seems deserted. I hesitate, wondering if Min is here after all, if she's already left.

No one is around to stop me from going in, so I decide to run over to the area where the Marriage Market is held and see if Min and Wei are there. The quiet is eerie, and I hear insects buzzing, something I've never heard in the city before.

When I come out the other side of the ornamental bridge, my gaze is drawn upward to a fluttering display above the path. I stop to take in the sight. For at least fifty meters, widely spaced clotheslines crisscross overhead.

Min's photos of women hang from the lines with their statements interspersed. They're strung low enough that I can read the words written in large red characters and see the warm, strong expression of each woman as I begin to move under the exhibit. Their faces are glowing and vibrant, set against solid colored backgrounds and strewn from tree to tree, giving the whole exhibit the effect of Tibetan prayer flags, rippling in the wind.

It takes my breath away that Min herself has imagined this, shot all the photos, produced all the pieces and executed such a stunning display. I realize that I had a small part to play in it, and tears spring to my eyes.

With the hard events of the day catching up to me and seeing Min's vision carried through, I'm no longer able to dam up my emotions. I want to admire each woman and reread every statement to shore myself up, but I hear voices ahead and remember what I've come for.

As I emerge at the end of the exhibit, someone shouts, "Wait! Stop there!" I halt and squint into the darkness of the park searching for Min; I'm sure it was her voice. A flash bursts from a tree. I'm briefly blinded, but after a moment I make out Wei standing under a tree, and Min straddling a branch above him with her camera aimed at the exhibit. The camera flashes a few more times before she calls out, "Thanks, Na! You can move now."

She hands Wei her camera and climbs down as I approach. They're both grinning, clearly proud of this work.

"Min, you've done it! It's beautiful!" I say. "I didn't know you were so close to doing the installation."

"Well, I decided I needed to do it now. I made some changes with how I planned to display the photographs. Stringing them up is much less costly than what I was originally going to do."

"She had to be cheap, because she just rented her studio!" Wei says.

"That's wonderful!" I try to sound enthusiastic, though my heart sinks. This means she probably won't be able to loan me any cash.

"That's why I wanted to get the exhibit displayed now, even if it meant making do with just the rope. The photographs and statements are really the important parts anyway. And the publicity I hope it gets. I put out the press release a couple hours ago and I hope it gets some attention before the park officials take it all down."

"Take it down? After all your work!"

Min shrugs. "Probably. I didn't apply for a permit. I doubt the authorities would've approved it anyway. But if they remove it, I'll make sure to use that for publicity as well. So what did you need to talk to me about?" she asks.

I force a smile. I built it up in my mind that Min would be able to help me. "I've decided to go back to school." I try to sound resolute, but my plans are on shaky ground again. "Gilbert and I aren't going to get married after all."

"Oh!" Her eyes get round and inquisitive. I can see her trying to decide whether to congratulate me, extend her sympathies, or ask me what led to these decisions.

"Yes. I don't have time to go into it. I'm hoping to catch the 11:40 bus tonight," I say to head off her questions. "I just wanted—to say goodbye." I turn to Wei. "And I was hoping to meet with you, too." I drop my bag and crouch to pull out Bao-bao's drawings. "I brought these back with me."

Wei reaches for them and shuffles through the sheets, holding them up to the light of the lamppost. "Oh! They're so good! Min, look at them."

Min leans in to look over his shoulder, murmuring her admiration as he goes through them again. She cocks her head at me thoughtfully. "Na, are you sure you want to pass these on?"

"Yes. He did them for Wei, and I still have his sketchbook." I press my lips together, hating to ask for payment, but it has to be done. "Besides, I need the money."

Wei's head jerks up and he gives me a look of surprise. "Na, I guess I didn't mention it before, because it didn't matter after what happened, but I already paid Bao-bao for these. I gave him the money up front."

"Oh." My shoulders slump. That never occurred to me.

Wei pats at his pockets. He brings out a wad of bills and smooths them out. "Take this—twenty-two yuan. I just paid my rent, so I don't have more on me."

"No, no," I protest and push away the money. "You already paid for them."

"If you need it, you need it. You can always pay me back one day." He pushes it into my hand and I take it, promising to pay him back.

"I wish I could help you out too," Min adds, "but the studio . . ."

"It's okay. I'll manage." I'm not sure how, but I know I have enough to at least get on the bus. I'm eager to go now. My mind is already scrambling. I need to get my other things from the apartment. I want to be on the bus before I lose my nerve, or before Mama decides to come back to Taiyuan.

What happened to Bao-bao comes rushing back to me. I squeeze my eyes shut against the truth.

"Na, are you okay?"

Yes is the reflexive answer that forms in my mouth, but Min looks so concerned, I catch myself before I say it. Of course, I can't tell her about Mama and Baba, or about Gilbert. Although I'm sure I can trust Min, their secrets aren't mine to expose.

"I'm going to be fine," I tell Min. "I have to hurry, though. Text me how it goes tomorrow!" I stuff the money into my pocket, pick up my bag, and say goodbye. I walk through the installation again, gazing up at the shimmering women as I pass, spurred on by their bold and heartfelt words.

◆ ◆ ◆

On the way to the apartment, my phone vibrates in my hand. I glance at it reflexively and halt when I see that it's Nainai. For a second, I don't want to answer it, certain that Mama has pressured her to call me and is hovering at her shoulder—or has taken Nainai's phone and is using it herself. But I hate to think of Nainai, of all people, staying up so late, worrying about me.

I click to answer, but in case Mama is on the other end, I don't say anything.

"Na?"

I exhale, relieved. "Yes, Nainai, I'm here."

She lets out a rush of breath herself. "Where are you? Your mama and baba are frantic! You won't answer them?"

"I'm okay, Nainai."

"I went to Gilbert's earlier this evening looking for you. He told me you broke it off! He wouldn't say why, only that you changed your mind, that it was up to you to explain if you wanted." Her voice is urgent, but soft. I sense that she's alone, maybe standing outside whispering into the phone so Mama won't hear.

"It's not going to work out." I perch on the edge of a concrete planter full of shrubs. The dark street is quiet and I can hear her breaths as silence falls between us. I know she wants to know the rest, but more than anyone, Nainai understands not to push when I'm not ready to talk.

"It's all right," she finally says. "Doesn't matter. Just come home."

"No, Nainai. I'm not coming home." I shake my head even though she can't see me.

"Is it because of whatever happened with—with your parents this afternoon? Whatever they said to you, Na, they didn't mean it. They're just grief-stricken."

I can't reveal what I've learned about Bao-bao's death. Knowing what Baba did would destroy her. "Don't worry about me. I'll be okay." I hold back from telling her anything—where I am, where I'm going—she'll have to share with Mama. "I have to go. But it's good to . . . hear your voice."

"Na!" Nainai says. "Whatever you argued with them

about—they'll come around. The old ways are hard to change, but not impossible."

"I'll call you soon," I tell her, my chest tightening as I click off.

✿ ✿ ✿

Talking to Nainai has given me one more idea about where to get my tuition money. I scan the alleys between the buildings and keep my ears attuned for the clatter of junk being tossed out of trash bins. Finally, when I'm a few blocks away from our building, I spot Mrs. Hu with her cart in an alley.

"Hello!" I shout to get her attention and run over.

"I thought you were going home for your brother's burial," she says.

"I did." I pause, torn about what exactly to say next. The lights in the alley throw shadows on her face, but her gaze is on me, solemn and expectant. I suddenly realize that she knows. She's known all along what happened to Bao-bao.

The last few hours evaporate, and once again, I'm back at Bao-bao's grave, flooded with the truth.

"Mrs. Hu, I know what happened to Bao-bao." I swallow the rest of the words on my tongue—Baba killed him and Mama covered it up.

"They told you," she says.

"It came out."

Mrs. Hu shakes her head grimly and looks up at the gray-black sky. "They're suffering."

My face twists with contempt. I don't know what to do with the awfulness of the truth. The words *They killed him* jump back into my mouth, needing to be spat out, but I can't say them.

"They—they—stole his youth!" I sputter fiercely, enraged for my brother, for myself. I bury my face in my hands, my fingers pressing over my closed lids as I try to stop up the hot tears that I can't hold back anymore.

Mrs. Hu's thick, rough fingers wrap gently around my wrists. She pulls my hands down and steers me over to sit on her cart stacked with tied bundles of newspapers. My tears gush out, running down my face and dripping onto my lap. I clutch my arms in my lap and bend over them, crying, sobbing, for several minutes, not bothering to wipe away the tears.

Finally, after my tears start to slow, Mrs. Hu speaks. "It's true. They stole his youth without meaning to. This is how they showed their love. They thought they were doing their best for him, and an accident of the worst kind happened. It was an accident, you understand. You have to know that."

I swipe at my face with the back of my hand. "But if they hadn't pushed him, tried to control him—if they let had him do what he wanted—"

"Parents aren't used to thinking that way. We do what we know."

"But Baba hit him! Killed him. And they covered it up!"

"The drinking, the hitting, was very, very bad, yes. How it came to that . . ." Mrs. Hu woefully shakes her head. "But your ba didn't know your brother struck his head. Bao-bao probably had some sort of internal bleeding." She grimaces before she continues. "He was cold when your mama found him after she got home. As soon as I got there, I knew it was too late to call the hospital."

My hands grip the stack of newspapers I'm sitting on. My heart is beating strangely in my chest and seems to echo off the cement walls of the two buildings. Mrs. Hu has paused, staring off, picturing that night, I'm sure. I stay very still so as not to distract her from her train of thought. She has more to tell me, and I know that I need to hear it.

"I saw right away how it would go if there was an inquest—your ba in trouble, a trial with press, probably prison. Your family would have been ruined. And nothing good would've come out of it. Your parents had already lost their child." She closes her eyes briefly and swallows, terrible grief on her face. Remembering her own son again.

"Believe me," she continues when she collects herself, "there is no worse thing. But to have all those problems on top of it, they didn't need that. They wouldn't have been able to stand that. At the time your parents didn't care about anything. They could hardly put two words together. It was all I could do to find out what had happened."

My tears have stopped. Mrs. Hu's hands are gripped together. She brings them up and rests her chin on them briefly.

"My eye fell on the rat poison your mama had just brought home with her. I took the box and tore it open. It was me who . . . *arranged* everything."

She looks at me with the oddest expression, frank and obdurate, with no regret for the part she played in hiding the truth. But watchful too, waiting for my reaction. I can only stare at her.

"I told your parents to let me explain it all. They were so lost in suffering. I called the police officer I know well from our neighborhood circuit. Gave him 2500 yuan to take care of the coroner. When the coroner arrived, I told them about the test scores. News about suicides always spikes up around testing time, so it wasn't an unreasonable conclusion." Mrs. Hu exhales, low and deep.

Mama's debt, Min's doubt, Mrs. Hu saying *they were just trying to help him.* It's as if the last piece of a puzzle has finally clicked into place.

A silence settles between us. My head drops and my gaze lands on a crack in the cement between my feet. I don't feel anything, can't think anything. All the fury and horror have left me. The air is thick and humid. The alley smells of garbage and urine. A dull echo sounds from the back of the building. I imagine it's Mr. Hu sorting the recyclables.

"Now you really know everything," Mrs. Hu says. "What are you going to do?"

What am I going to do? I stand up and pace the alley.

Baba still killed Bao-bao.

An accident.

And Mrs. Hu helped them cover it up.

She did it out of compassion.

Nothing would be better if my parents were held legally responsible for Bao-bao's death.

But how does knowing all that change what I'm going to do next? I picture myself going back to work with Mama at the plant, going home to the dark apartment. Day in, day out. My breath is short and quick with the suffocating notion. What will be different?

"Mrs. Hu." I steady my breath before I turn toward her. "I'm sorry to ask when we've just started to pay our debt to you, but I came here tonight to see if you would loan me 350 yuan. I want to go back to school."

Mrs. Hu purses her lips. I'm afraid she's going to say no.

"I can't stay here. I can't help them." My voice is calm. I'm surprised at my detached, level tone. "I've been trying all summer to help them, to be compliant and good, to take Bao-bao's place, but it's too late for us to have that kind of relationship. I've been on my own all these years, and I just know I have to go back to school now."

Her head bobs slowly. "The money is no problem. I'll give you the money. But have you told your parents what you want to do?"

I shake my head miserably. They've never considered what Bao-bao wanted, much less what I wanted. Like Mrs. Hu said, they don't know how to do that. Even if I can get past what Baba did to Bao-bao, I don't see how we will ever be able to relate to each other—or how I'll ever be able to trust them again.

"The worst thing has already happened to them," Mrs. Hu says. "They won't want to lose another child. Give them a chance."

29

Mrs. Hu takes me back to our building and loans me the money for my tuition. I go down to my apartment to get the rest of my things, but when I see the bed, I fall into the cool striped sheets. I let the 11:40 p.m. bus to Linfen go without me, and instead, I sleep and sleep.

In the morning the soft pinging of a text on my phone wakes me. I lean over and dig it out of my bag on the floor. The message is from Min: the photo she took of me last night standing under her exhibit, my long hair caped around my shoulders, still showing the ripples from my unbound braid. My face is tilted upward, my eyes looking plainly ahead. I don't remember smiling, and maybe it was a trick of the flash, but there I am, looking surprisingly confident, surprisingly at peace, under the fluttering banner of radiant women.

There are more texts from Mama, the ones I ignored last night. I don't bother to read them, but I forward the photograph of me to her and begin to type.

Mama, I'm going back to school today . . .

AUTHOR'S NOTE

After researching my first novel, *Girls on the Line*, I was struck by how China's rapid modernization has affected the country's young people. Confucian values and an authoritarian government have bred an admirable collectivistic society, but many young people wrestle with the problems and pressures of a deeply felt responsibility to family and society, often at the expense of their true selves. I have no doubt that Chinese society will continue to change and flourish. This novel aims only to highlight the struggles of one moment, one generation, in this culture.

China's notorious National Higher Education Entrance Exam, nicknamed gaokao, *high exam*, is the country's single determinant for entrance into universities and colleges. With 9.8 million students (according to 2018 statistics) competing for spots based solely on their gaokao rankings, competition is fierce. Knowing that higher education is the only way up, parents begin to chivvy their children towards academic excellence as early as preschool.

Due to China's strict household registration system, which limits free education and healthcare outside of one's home locale, an estimated 61 million children are *left-behind*, living in the countryside as parents migrate to cities for work. Most of these children live with grandparents, although an estimated 2 million live alone. In many cases, left-behind children have linked the absence of their parents to feelings of abandonment, low self-esteem, anxiety, and depression.

A 2014 report by a Chinese nonprofit organization, 21st Century Education Research Institute, identified suicide as the leading cause of death for youth. Because the Chinese government does not release statistics on suicide, the organization sources information from online posts and media reports. An overwhelming percent of the cases it found were linked to academic stress. The organization's 2017 report also mentions family issues, disputes with teachers, and other interpersonal problems in the cases studied.

Some experts believe pressure from family and feelings of isolation contribute to the mental health problems of Chinese youth, most of whom grow up as singletons and can struggle to handle difficult interpersonal interactions.

Young single women, especially those who are well educated, face powerful family and societal pressures to marry. In 2007, the same year the government identified the gender imbalance created by China's One-Child Policy as cause for concern, state-run media began widely disseminating the term *shengnu*—"leftovers"—into the mainstream. This kind of rhetoric essentially stigmatizes unmarried women over 27 years old and pressures women to marry and have children earlier rather than focusing on their careers.

While young people in China are growing up in a much different country than their parents, traditional Confucian values remain vital. Respect for one's parents still runs strong, and it is still widely considered desirable to get married and have a child.

Stigma and the pressure to conform also extend to

the gay population in China. Although homosexuality was decriminalized in China in 1997 and declassified as a mental disorder in 2001, the unofficial government policy is often expressed by the Chinese idiom, *not encouraging, not discouraging and not promoting.* With neither support to rely on nor open persecution to rebel against, the LGBTQ+ experience is painfully isolating, and understanding and acceptance of LGBTQ+ issues remain uncommon, especially in rural areas. No firm statistics are available, but experts estimate that only 3–5 percent of the country's 40–70 million LGBTQ+ individuals are out of the closet, and as many as 80 percent of China's gay men marry women.

Despite the rapid transformation of China's economic status, traditional social structures and thinking persist on a large scale. However, changes are emerging with the rise of educated youth, more progressive attitudes in urban areas, and the Internet—where, despite censorship, online communities serve as a refuge, a resource, and the seat of burgeoning activism. The government has taken small steps to research and address problems: China's first mental health law was enacted in 2012; three ministries are conducting a joint survey to improve conditions for left-behind children; a reform of the gaokao system will be implemented in 2020 to allow more equal access to higher education for the rural population; and in 2012, three female activists wearing red-spattered white wedding gowns marched through a Beijing shopping district to raise awareness about domestic abuse, inspiring a small but growing feminist movement in China.

ACKNOWLEDGMENTS

I'm so grateful for my conscientious and supportive first readers Ann Howell, Linda Steitler, Williamaye Jones, Annice Brown, as well as my mentor P.B. Parris. Also thanks to Shannon Hassan, amazing agent, and Amy Fitzgerald, editor, whose words are always thought provoking. Thanks to Libby Stille, publicist, and Emily Harris for the gorgeous book design.

I read so many excellent articles and nonfiction titles that fed the backdrop for this story. For further reading about the issues young people are facing in China, I especially recommend the following nonfiction books: *Young China* by Zak Dychtwald, *Wish Lanterns* by Alec Ash, *Leftover Women* by Leta Hong Fincher, *Little Soldiers* by Lenora Chu, and *Under Red Skies* by Karoline Kan.

TOPICS FOR DISCUSSION

1. Why does Na resent Bao-bao? How did their relationship change after their parents took Bao-bao to the city?

2. How do traditional Chinese attitudes about children's duty to their parents shape Na's and Gilbert's ideas about what they can do with their lives? How has Bao-bao pushed back against these attitudes?

3. Na's family has a limited understanding of depression and other mental health issues. How might this make it difficult for Na's parents to understand the possible effects of the various pressures they've put on their children?

4. Describe Na's relationship with her parents. In what ways do her parents show that they love her? How does this compare to the ways your family shows affection?

5. How are Min and Wei different from anyone Na has met before? What does she learn about her brother through them?

6. Na's father says that having a daughter is *like spilled water*— a waste—because a daughter will inevitably leave her family when she marries. What other kinds of waste does Na see happening in her family? What scenarios would feel *like spilled water* to her?

7. Why is Na initially uncertain about whether to accept Gilbert's proposal? What advantages would marriage give her? What limitations would it impose on her?

8. How does working on Min's project affect Na's perspective on marriage?

9. Na believes that she's nothing like the unconventional heroine of Charlotte Brontë's novel *Jane Eyre*. But in what ways does Na defy society's expectations for her?

10. How is the pressure on Gilbert to marry a woman and conceal his orientation similar to the pressures Na and Bao-bao have faced? How is it different?

11. Mrs. Hu wants Na to give her parents a second chance and forgive them for what happened to Bao-bao. Do you agree with Mrs. Hu? Why or why not?

12. What questions does the end of the novel leave open-ended? How do you think these issues will play out over the next few years of Na's life?

ABOUT THE AUTHOR

Jennie Liu is the daughter of Chinese immigrants. Having been brought up with an ear to two cultures, she has been fascinated by the attitudes, social policies, and changes in China each time she visits. She lives in North Carolina with her husband and two boys. She is also the author of the young adult novel *Girls on the Line*.